KU-687-649

The
Storytellers
One

Compiled by

Roger Mansfield

Illustrated by Brian Lee

SCHOFIELD & SIMS LTD HUDDERSFIELD

0 7217 0229 5

First printed 1971
Reprinted 1971
Reprinted (Twice) 1972
Reprinted 1973
Reprinted 1974
Reprinted 1976
Reprinted 1977
Reprinted 1978

The Storytellers is a series of two books:

The Storytellers One   0 7217 0229 5
The Storytellers Two   0 7217 0230 9

ACKNOWLEDGMENTS

The author and publishers wish to thank the following for permission to use
copyright material:

Martin Secker & Warburg Ltd., for *Higher Standards* by Angus Wilson from
A Bit off the Map.

W. H. Allen & Co. Ltd., for *The Other John Peel* by Alan Sillitoe.

Mrs. Judith Wright McKinney, for her story *In the Park*.

Curtis Brown Ltd., for *The Leader of the People* by John Steinbeck from
The Long Valley, and *No Witchcraft for Sale* by Doris Lessing from
This was the Old Chief's Country.

George G. Harrap & Co. Ltd., for *Spit Nolan* by Bill Naughton.

A. D. Peters & Company, for *A Sound of Thunder* by Ray Bradbury; reprinted
by permission.

Printed in England by Henry Garnett and Company Limited, Rotherham and London.

Contents

Bill Naughton

Bill Naughton was born in County Mayo, Ireland in 1910, but not long afterwards his parents moved to England, to Bolton in Lancashire, where he lived for many years. After leaving school at fourteen, he took his first job, as an apprentice weaver in a local mill; later he worked as a coal-bagger and a lorry driver. In the years of the Depression when he was often 'on the dole', he spent the time in public libraries educating himself. Writing did not come easily to him but during the Second World War he began to produce short stories for magazines and by the end of the war he was successful enough to make his living by full-time writing. It was not until the late 1950's, however, that he became widely known, although he tries to avoid the publicity and 'most of the social carry-on' that accompany fame.

His childhood in Bolton and his experiences as a manual worker still provide much of the material for his stories; written in a lively, colloquial style, and concerned mainly with ordinary working class people these display an unusual warmth and humour. They include: *The Goalkeeper's Revenge*, a collection of short stories 'for boys and about boys', from which 'Spit Nolan' (*Storytellers 1*) is taken; another collection, *Late Night on Watling Street*, the title story of which appears in *Storytellers 2*; and *One Small Boy*, a novel about a family who leave the west coast of Ireland to settle in Lancashire. He has also written several plays, the best known of which is probably *Alfie*—this was first a radio play and was then adapted as a stage play, a film and a novel. *Spring and Port Wine* and *All in Good Time* are another two plays which have been filmed (the latter as *The Family Way*).

Spit Nolan

SPIT NOLAN was a pal of mine. He was a thin lad with a bony face that was always pale, except for two rosy spots on his cheekbones. He had quick brown eyes, short, wiry hair, rather stooped shoulders, and we all knew that he had only one lung. He had a disease which in those days couldn't be cured unless you went away to Switzerland, which Spit certainly couldn't afford. He wasn't sorry for himself in any way, and in fact we envied him, because he never had to go to school.

Spit was the champion trolley-rider of Cotton Pocket; that was the district in which we lived. He had a very good balance, and sharp wits, and he was very brave, so that these qualities, when added to his skill as a rider, meant that no other boy could ever beat Spit on a trolley—and every lad had one.

Our trolleys were simple vehicles for getting a good ride downhill at a fast speed. To make one you had to get a stout piece of wood about five feet in length and eighteen inches wide. Then you needed four wheels, preferably two pairs, large ones for the back and smaller ones for the front. However, since we bought our wheels from the scrapyard, most trolleys had four odd wheels. Now you had to get a poker and put it in the fire until it was red hot, and then burn a hole through the wood at the front. Usually it would take three or four attempts to get the hole bored through. Through this hole you fitted the giant nut-and-bolt, which acted as a swivel for the steering. Fastened to the nut was a strip of wood,

5

on to which the front axle was secured by bent nails. A piece of rope tied to each end of the axle served for steering. Then a knob of margarine had to be slanced out of the kitchen to grease the wheels and bearings. Next you had to paint a name on it: *Invincible* or *Dreadnought*, though it might be a motto: *Death before Dishonour* or *Labour and Wait*. That done, you then stuck your chest out, opened the back gate, and wheeled your trolley out to face the critical eyes of the world.

Spit spent most mornings trying out new speed gadgets on his trolley, or searching Enty's scrapyard for good wheels. Afternoons he would go off and have a spin down Cemetery Brew. This was a very steep road that led to the cemetery, and it was very popular with trolley-drivers as it was the only macadamised hill for miles around, all the others being cobblestones for horse traffic. Spit used to lie in wait for a coal-cart or other horse-drawn vehicle, then he would hitch *Egdam* to the back to take it up the brew.

Egdam was a name in memory of a girl called Madge, whom he had once met at Southport Sanatorium, where he had spent three happy weeks. Only I knew the meaning of it, for he had reversed the letters of her name to keep his love a secret.

It was the custom for lads to gather at the street corner on summer evenings and, trolleys parked at hand, discuss trolleying, road surfaces, and also show off any new gadgets. Then, when Spit gave the sign, we used to set off for Cemetery Brew. There was scarcely any evening traffic on the roads in those days, so that we could have a good practice before our evening race. Spit, the unbeaten champion, would inspect every trolley and rider, and allow a start which was reckoned on the size of the wheels and the weight of the rider. He was always the last in the line of starters, though no matter how long a start he gave it seemed impossible to beat him. He knew that road like the palm of his hand, every tiny lump or pothole, and he never came a cropper.

Among us he took things easy, but when occasion asked for it he would go all out. Once he had to meet a challenge from Ducker Smith, the champion of the Engine Row gang. On that occasion Spit borrowed a wheel from the baby's pram, removing one nearest the wall, so it wouldn't be missed, and confident he could replace it before his mother took baby out. And after fixing it to his trolley he made that ride in what was called the 'belly-down' style—that is, he lay full stretch on his stomach, so as to avoid wind resistance. Although Ducker got away with a flying start he had not that sensitive touch of Spit, and his frequent bumps and swerves lost him valuable inches, so that he lost the race with a good three lengths. Spit arrived home just in time to catch his mother as she was wheeling young Georgie off the doorstep, and if he had not made a dash for it the child would have fallen out as the pram overturned.

It happened that we were gathered at the street corner with our

7

trolleys one evening when Ernie Haddock let out a hiccup of wonder: 'Hy, chaps, wot's Leslie got?'

We all turned our eyes on Leslie Duckett, the plump son of the local publican. He approached us on a brand-new trolley, propelled by flicks of his foot on the pavement. From a distance the thing had looked impressive, but now, when it came up among us, we were too dumbfounded to speak. Such a magnificent trolley had never been seen! The riding board was of solid oak, almost two inches thick; four new wheels with pneumatic tyres; a brake, a bell, a lamp, and a spotless steering-cord. In front was a plate on which was the name in bold lettering: *The British Queen*.

'It's called after the pub,' remarked Leslie. He tried to edge it away from Spit's trolley, for it made *Egdam* appear horribly insignificant. Voices had been stilled for a minute, but now they broke out:

'Where'd it come from?'

'How much was it?'

'Who made it?'

Leslie tried to look modest. 'My dad had it specially made to measure,' he said, 'by the gaffer of the Holt Engineering Works.'

He was a nice lad, and now he wasn't sure whether to feel proud or ashamed. The fact was, nobody had ever had a trolley made by somebody else. Trolleys were swopped and so on, but no lad had ever owned one that had been made by other hands. We went quiet now, for Spit had calmly turned his attention to it, and was examining *The British Queen* with his expert eye. First he tilted it, so that one of the rear wheels was off the ground, and after giving it a flick of the finger he listened intently with his ear close to the hub.

'A beautiful ball-bearing race,' he remarked, 'it runs like silk.' Next he turned his attention to the body. 'Grand piece of timber, Leslie—though a trifle on the heavy side. It'll take plenty of pulling up a brew.'

'I can pull it,' said Leslie, stiffening.

'You might find it a shade *front-heavy*,' went on Spit, 'which means it'll be hard on the steering unless you keep it well oiled.'

'It's well made,' said Leslie. 'Eh, Spit ?'

Spit nodded. 'Aye, all the bolts are counter sunk,' he said, 'everything chamfered and fluted off to perfection. But—'

'But what ?' asked Leslie.

'Do you want me to tell you ?' asked Spit.

'Yes, I do,' answered Leslie.

'Well, it's got none of *you* in it,' said Spit.

'How do you mean ?' says Leslie.

'Well, you haven't so much as given it a single tap with a hammer,' said Spit. 'That trolley will be a stranger to you to your dying day.'

'How come,' said Leslie, 'since I *own* it ?'

Spit shook his head. 'You don't own it,' he said, in a quiet, solemn tone. 'You own nothing in this world except those things you have taken a hand in the making of, or else you've earned the money to buy them.'

Leslie sat down on *The British Queen* to think this one out. We all sat round, scratching our heads.

'You've forgotten to mention one thing,' said Ernie Haddock to Spit, 'what about the *speed* ?'

'Going down a steep hill,' said Spit, 'she should hold the road well—an' with wheels like that she should certainly be able to shift some.'

'Think she could beat *Egdam* ?' ventured Ernie.

'That,' said Spit, 'remains to be seen.'

Ernie gave a shout: 'A challenge race! *The British Queen* versus *Egdam* !'

'Not tonight,' said Leslie. 'I haven't got the proper feel of her yet.'

'What about Sunday morning ?' I said.

9

Spit nodded. 'As good a time as any.'

Leslie agreed. 'By then,' he said in a challenging tone, 'I'll be able to handle her.'

Chattering like monkeys, eating bread, carrots, fruit, and bits of toffee, the entire gang of us made our way along the silent Sunday-morning streets for the big race at Cemetery Brew. We were split into two fairly equal sides.

Leslie, in his serge Sunday suit, walked ahead, with Ernie Haddock pulling *The British Queen*, and a bunch of supporters around. They were optimistic, for Leslie had easily outpaced every other trolley during the week, though as yet he had not run against Spit.

Spit was in the middle of the group behind, and I was pulling *Egdam* and keeping the pace easy, for I wanted Spit to keep fresh. He walked in and out among us with an air of imperturbability that, considering the occasion, seemed almost godlike. It inspired a fanatical confidence in us. It was such that Chick Dale, a curly-headed kid with soft skin like a girl's, and a nervous lisp, climbed up on to the spiked railings of the cemetery, and, reaching out with his thin fingers, snatched a yellow rose. He ran in front of Spit and thrust it into a small hole in his jersey.

'I pwesent you with the wose of the winner!' he exclaimed.

'And I've a good mind to present you with a clout on the lug,' replied Spit, 'for pinching a flower from a cemetery. An' what's more, it's bad luck.' Seeing Chick's face, he relented. 'On second thoughts, Chick, I'll wear it. Ee, wot a 'eavenly smell!'

Happily we went along, and Spit turned to a couple of lads at the back. 'Hy, stop that whistling. Don't forget what day it is—folk want their sleep out.'

A faint sweated glow had come over Spit's face when we reached the top of the hill, but he was as majestically calm as ever. Taking the bottle of cold water from his trolley seat, he put it to his lips and rinsed out his mouth in the manner of a boxer.

The two contestants were called together by Ernie.

'No bumpin' or borin',' he said.

They nodded.

'The winner,' he said, 'is the first who puts the nose of his trolley past the cemetery gates.'

They nodded.

'Now, who,' he asked, 'is to be judge?'

Leslie looked at me. 'I've no objection to Bill,' he said. 'I know he's straight.'

I hadn't realised I was, I thought, but by heck I will be!

'Ernie here,' said Spit, 'can be starter.'

With that Leslie and Spit shook hands.

'Fly down to them gates,' said Ernie to me. He had his father's pigeon-timing watch in his hand. 'I'll be setting 'em off dead on the stroke of ten o'clock.'

I hurried down to the gates. I looked back and saw the

supporters lining themselves on either side of the road. Leslie was sitting upright on *The British Queen*. Spit was settling himself to ride belly-down. Ernie Haddock, handkerchief raised in the right hand, eye gazing down on the watch in the left, was counting them off—just like when he tossed one of his father's pigeons.

'Five—four—three—two—one—*Off!*'

Spit was away like a shot. That vigorous toe push sent him clean ahead of Leslie. A volley of shouts went up from his supporters, and groans from Leslie's. I saw Spit move straight to the middle of the road camber. Then I ran ahead to take up my position at the winning post.

When I turned again I was surprised to see that Spit had not increased the lead. In fact, it seemed that Leslie had begun to gain on him. He had settled himself into a crouched position, and those perfect wheels combined with his extra weight were bringing him up with Spit. Not that it seemed possible he could ever catch him. For Spit, lying flat on his trolley, moving with a fine balance, gliding, as it were, over the rough patches, looked to me as though he were a bird that might suddenly open out its wings and fly clean in to the air.

The runners along the side could no longer keep up with the trolleys. And now, as they skimmed past the half-way mark, and came to the very steepest part, there was no doubt that Leslie was gaining. Spit had never ridden better; he coaxed *Egdam* over the tricky parts, swayed with her, gave her her head, and guided her. Yet Leslie, clinging grimly to the steering-rope of *The British Queen*, and riding the rougher part of the road, was actually drawing level. Those beautiful ball-bearing wheels, engineer-made, encased in oil, were holding the road, and bringing Leslie along faster than spirit and skill could carry Spit.

Dead level they sped into the final stretch. Spit's slight figure was poised fearlessly on his trolley, drawing the extremes of speed from her. Thundering beside him, anxious but determined, came

Leslie. He was actually drawing ahead—and forcing his way to the top of the camber. On they came like two charioteers—Spit delicately edging to the side, to gain inches by the extra downward momentum. I kept my eyes fastened clean across the road as they came belting past the winning-post.

First past was the plate *The British Queen*. I saw that first. Then I saw the heavy rear wheel jog over a pothole and strike Spit's front wheel—sending him in a swerve across the road. Suddenly then, from nowhere, a charabanc came speeding round the wide bend.

Spit was straight in its path. Nothing could avoid the collision. I gave a cry of fear as I saw the heavy solid tyre of the front wheel hit the trolley. Spit was flung up and his back hit the radiator. Then the driver stopped dead.

I got there first. Spit was lying on the macadam road on his side. His face was white and dusty, and coming out between his lips and trickling down his chin was a rivulet of fresh red blood. Scattered all about him were yellow rose petals.

'Not my fault,' I heard the driver shouting. 'I didn't have a chance. He came straight at me.'

The next thing we were surrounded by women who had got out of the charabanc. And then Leslie and all the lads came up.

'Somebody send for an ambulance!' called a woman.

'I'll run an' tell the gatekeeper to telephone,' said Ernie Haddock.

'I hadn't a chance,' the driver explained to the women.

'A piece of his jersey on the starting-handle there . . . ' said someone.

'Don't move him,' said the driver to a stout woman who had bent over Spit. 'Wait for the ambulance.'

'Hush up,' she said. She knelt and put a silk scarf under Spit's head. Then she wiped his mouth with her little handkerchief.

He opened his eyes. Glazed they were, as though he couldn't

see. A short cough came out of him, then he looked at me and his lips moved.

'*Who won?*'

'Thee!' blurted out Leslie. 'Tha just licked me. Eh, Bill?'

'Aye,' I said, 'old *Egdam* just pipped *The British Queen*.'

Spit's eyes closed again. The women looked at each other. They nearly all had tears in their eyes. Then Spit looked up again, and his wise, knowing look came over his face. After a minute he spoke in a sharp whisper:

'Liars. I can remember seeing Leslie's back wheel hit my front 'un. I didn't win—I lost.' He stared upward for a few seconds, then his eyes twitched and shut.

The driver kept repeating how it wasn't his fault, and next thing the ambulance came. Nearly all the women were crying now, and I saw the look that went between the two men who put Spit on a stretcher—but I couldn't believe he was dead. I had to go into the ambulance with the attendant to give him particulars. I went up the step and sat down inside and looked out the little window as the driver slammed the doors. I saw the driver holding Leslie as a witness. Chick Dale was lifting the smashed-up *Egdam* on to the body of *The British Queen*. People with bunches of flowers in their hands stared after us as we drove off. Then I heard the ambulance man asking me Spit's name. Then he touched me on the elbow with his pencil and said:

'Where *did* he live?'

I knew then. That word 'did' struck right into me. But for a minute I couldn't answer. I had to think hard, for the way he said it made it suddenly seem as though Spit Nolan had been dead and gone for ages.

BILL NAUGHTON

Doris Lessing

Doris Lessing was born in Persia in 1919. Shortly afterwards her father went to Rhodesia, and she was brought up on a large farm there; she attended school in Salisbury. In 1949 she arrived in England with a small son to care for, very little money, and the manuscript of her first novel, *The Grass is Singing*. This fortunately was accepted almost at once and was published in 1950. It was followed a year later by a collection of short stories entitled *This Was the Old Chief's Country*, from which both 'No Witchcraft for Sale' (*Storytellers 1*) and 'Sunrise on the Veld' (*Storytellers 2*) are taken. In these, as in most of her work, the plot is relatively unimportant. Instead she concentrates on capturing ordinary but nevertheless significant moments in a person's life.

Although she now resides in England, many of her stories are still set in South Africa or Rhodesia, where she lived for twenty-five years. In 1954 she was presented with the Somerset Maugham Award for the promise of her writing in general, and the high standard of her fourth book—*Five—Short Novels*—in particular. Another volume of short stories which received high praise was *The Habit of Loving* (1957).

No Witchcraft For Sale

THE Farquars had been childless for years when little Teddy was born; and they were touched by the pleasure of their servants, who brought presents of fowls and eggs and flowers to the homestead when they came to rejoice over the baby, exclaiming with delight over his downy golden head and his blue eyes. They congratulated Mrs. Farquar as if she had achieved a very great thing, and she felt that she had—her smile for the lingering, admiring natives was warm and grateful.

Later, when Teddy had his first haircut, Gideon the cook picked up the soft gold tufts from the ground, and held them reverently in his hand. Then he smiled at the little boy and said: 'Little Yellow Head.' That became the native name for the child. Gideon and Teddy were great friends from the first. When Gideon had finished his work, he would lift Teddy on his shoulders to the shade of a big tree, and play with him there, forming curious little toys from twigs and leaves and grass, or shaping animals from wetted soil. When Teddy learned to walk it was often Gideon who crouched before him, clucking encouragement, finally catching him when he fell, tossing him up in the air till they both became breathless with laughter. Mrs. Farquar was fond of the old cook because of his love for her child.

There was no second baby; and one day Gideon said: 'Ah, missus, missus, the Lord above sent this one; Little Yellow Head is the most good thing we have in our house.' Because of that 'we'

Mrs. Farquar felt a warm impulse towards her cook; and at the end of the month she raised his wages. He had been with her now for several years; he was one of the few natives who had his wife and children in the compound and never wanted to go home to his kraal, which was some hundreds of miles away. Sometimes a small piccanin, who had been born the same time as Teddy, could be seen peering from the edge of the bush, staring in awe at the little white boy with his miraculous fair hair and northern blue eyes. The two little children would gaze at each other with a wide interested gaze, and once Teddy put out his hand curiously to touch the black child's cheeks and hair.

Gideon, who was watching, shook his head wonderingly, and said: 'Ah, missus, these are both children, and one will grow up to be a Baas, and one will be a servant'; and Mrs. Farquar smiled and said sadly, 'Yes, Gideon, I was thinking the same.' She sighed. 'It is God's will,' said Gideon, who was a mission boy. The Farquars were very religious people; and this shared feeling about God bound servant and masters even closer together.

Teddy was about six years old when he was given a scooter, and discovered the intoxications of speed. All day he would fly around the homestead, in and out of flowerbeds, scattering squawking chickens and irritated dogs, finishing with a wide dizzying arc into the kitchen door. There he would cry: 'Gideon, look at me!' And Gideon would laugh and say: 'Very clever, Little Yellow Head.' Gideon's youngest son, who was now a herdsboy, came especially up from the compound to see the scooter. He was afraid to come near it, but Teddy showed off in front of him. 'Piccanin,' shouted Teddy, 'get out of my way!' And he raced in circles around the black child until he was frightened, and fled back to the bush.

'Why did you frighten him?' asked Gideon, gravely reproachful.

Teddy said defiantly: 'He's only a black boy,' and laughed.

Then, when Gideon turned away from him without speaking, his face fell. Very soon he slipped into the house and found an orange and brought it to Gideon, saying: 'This is for you.' He could not bring himself to say he was sorry; but he could not bear to lose Gideon's affection either. Gideon took the orange unwillingly and sighed. 'Soon you will be going away to school, Little Yellow Head,' he said wonderingly, 'and then you will be grown up.' He shook his head gently and said, 'And that is how our lives go.' He seemed to be putting a distance between himself and Teddy, not because of resentment, but in the way a person accepts something inevitable. The baby had lain in his arms and smiled up into his face: the tiny boy had swung from his shoulders, had played with him by the hour. Now Gideon would not let his flesh touch the flesh of the white child. He was kind, but there was a grave formality in his voice that made Teddy pout and sulk away. Also, it made him into a man: with Gideon he was polite, and carried himself formally, and if he came into the kitchen to ask for something, it was in the way a white man uses towards a servant, expecting to be obeyed.

But on the day that Teddy came staggering into the kitchen with his fists to his eyes, shrieking with pain, Gideon dropped the pot full of hot soup that he was holding, rushed to the child, and forced aside his fingers. 'A snake!' he exclaimed. Teddy had been on his scooter, and had come to a rest with his foot on the side of a big tub full of plants. A tree-snake, hanging by its tail from the roof, had spat full into his eyes. Mrs. Farquar came running when she heard the commotion. 'He'll go blind,' she sobbed, holding Teddy close against her. 'Gideon, he'll go blind!' Already the eyes, with perhaps half an hour's sight left in them, were swollen up to the size of fists: Teddy's small white face was distorted by great purple oozing protuberances. Gideon said: 'Wait a minute, missus, I'll get some medicine.' He ran off into the bush.

19

Mrs. Farquar lifted the child into the house and bathed his eyes with permanganate. She had scarcely heard Gideon's words; but when she saw that her remedies had no effect at all, and remembered how she had seen natives with no sight in their eyes, because of the spitting of a snake, she began to look for the return of her cook, remembering what she had heard of the efficacy of native herbs. She stood by the window, holding the terrified, sobbing little boy in her arms, and peered helplessly into the bush. It was not more than a few minutes before she saw Gideon come bounding back, and in his hand he held a plant.

'Do not be afraid, missus,' said Gideon, 'this will cure Little Yellow Head's eyes.' He stripped the leaves from the plant, leaving a small white fleshy root. Without even washing it, he put the root in his mouth, chewed it vigorously, and then held the spittle there while he took the child forcibly from Mrs. Farquar. He gripped Teddy down between his knees, and pressed the balls of his thumbs into the swollen eyes, so that the child screamed and Mrs. Farquar cried out in protest: 'Gideon, Gideon!' But Gideon took no notice. He knelt over the writhing child, pushing back the puffy lids till chinks of eyeball showed, and then he spat hard, again and again, into first one eye, and then the other. He finally lifted Teddy gently into his mother's arms, and said: 'His eyes will get better.' But Mrs. Farquar was weeping with terror, and she could hardly thank him: it was impossible to believe that Teddy could keep his sight. In a couple of hours the swellings were gone; the eyes were inflamed and tender but Teddy could see. Mr. and Mrs. Farquar went to Gideon in the kitchen and thanked him over and over again. They felt helpless because of their gratitude: it seemed they could do nothing to express it. They gave Gideon presents for his wife and children, and a big increase in wages, but these things could not pay for Teddy's now completely cured eyes. Mrs. Farquar said: 'Gideon, God chose you as an instrument for His goodness,' and Gideon said:

'Yes, missus, God is very good.'

Now, when such a thing happens on a farm, it cannot be long before everyone hears of it. Mr. and Mrs. Farquar told their neighbours and the story was discussed from one end of the district to the other. The bush is full of secrets. No one can live in Africa, or at least on the veld, without learning very soon that there is an ancient wisdom of leaf and soil and season—and, too, perhaps most important of all, of the darker tracts of the human mind—which is the black man's heritage. Up and down the district people were telling anecdotes, reminding each other of things that had happened to them.

'But I saw it myself, I tell you. It was a puff-adder bite. The kaffir's arm was swollen to the elbow, like a great shiny black bladder. He was groggy after half a minute. He was dying. Then suddenly a kaffir walked out of the bush with his hands full of green stuff. He smeared something on the place, and next day my boy was back at work, and all you could see was two small punctures in the skin.'

This was the kind of tale they told. And, as always, with a certain amount of exasperation, because while all of them knew that in the bush of Africa are waiting valuable drugs locked in bark, in simple-looking leaves, in roots, it was impossible to ever get the truth about them from the natives themselves.

The story eventually reached town; and perhaps it was at a sundowner party, or some such function, that a doctor, who happened to be there, challenged it. 'Nonsense,' he said. 'These things get exaggerated in the telling. We are always checking up on this kind of story, and we draw a blank every time.'

Anyway, one morning there arrived a strange car at the homestead, and out stepped one of the workers from the laboratory in town, with cases full of test-tubes and chemicals.

Mr. and Mrs. Farquar were flustered and pleased and flattered. They asked the scientist to lunch, and they told the story all over again, for the hundredth time. Little Teddy was there too, his blue eyes sparkling with health, to prove the truth of it. The scientist explained how humanity might benefit if this new drug could be offered for sale; and the Farquars were even more pleased: they were kind, simple people, who liked to think of something good coming about because of them. But when the scientist began talking of the money that might result, their manner showed discomfort. Their feelings over the miracle (that was how they thought of it) were so strong and deep and religious, that it was distasteful to them to think of money. The scientist, seeing their faces, went back to his first point, which was the advancement of humanity. He was perhaps a trifle perfunctory: it was not the first time he had come salting the tail of a fabulous bush-secret.

Eventually, when the meal was over, the Farquars called Gideon into their living-room and explained to him that this baas, here, was a Big Doctor from the Big City, and he had come all that way to see Gideon. At this Gideon seemed afraid; he did not understand; and Mrs. Farquar explained quickly that it was because of the wonderful thing he had done with Teddy's eyes that the Big Baas had come.

Gideon looked from Mrs. Farquar to Mr. Farquar, and then at the little boy, who was showing great importance because of the occasion. At last he said grudgingly: 'The Big Baas wants to know what medicine I used?' He spoke incredulously, as if he could not believe his old friends could so betray him. Mr. Farquar began explaining how a useful medicine could be made out of the root, and how it could be put on sale, and how thousands of people, black and white, up and down the continent of Africa, could be saved by the medicine when that spitting snake filled their eyes with poison. Gideon listened, his eyes bent on the ground, the skin of his forehead puckering in discomfort. When Mr. Farquar had finished he did not reply. The scientist, who all this time had been leaning back in a big chair, sipping his coffee and smiling with sceptical good-humour, chipped in and explained all over again, in different words, about the making of drugs and the progress of science. Also, he offered Gideon a present.

There was silence after this further explanation, and then Gideon remarked indifferently that he could not remember the root. His face was sullen and hostile, even when he looked at the Farquars, whom he usually treated like old friends. They were beginning to feel annoyed; and this feeling annulled the guilt that had been sprung into life by Gideon's accusing manner. They were beginning to feel that he was unreasonable. But it was at that moment that they all realised he would never give in. The magical drug would remain where it was, unknown and useless except for the tiny scattering of Africans who had the knowledge, natives who might be digging a ditch for the municipality in a ragged shirt and a pair of patched shorts, but who were still born to healing, hereditary healers, being the nephews or sons of the old witch doctors whose ugly masks and bits of bone and all the uncouth properties of magic were the outward signs of real power and wisdom.

The Farquars might tread on that plant fifty times a day as they passed from house to garden, from cow kraal to mealie field, but they would never know it.

But they went on persuading and arguing, with all the force of their exasperation; and Gideon continued to say that he could not remember, or that there was no such root, or that it was the wrong season of the year, or that it wasn't the root itself but the spittle from his mouth that had cured Teddy's eyes. He said all these things one after another, and seemed not to care they were contradictory. He was rude and stubborn. The Farquars could hardly recognise their gentle, lovable old servant in this ignorant, perversely obstinate native, standing there in front of them with lowered eyes, his hands twitching his cook's apron, repeating over and over whichever one of the stupid refusals that first entered his head.

And suddenly he appeared to give in. He lifted his head, gave a long, blank angry look at the circle of whites, who seemed to him like a circle of yelping dogs pressing around him, and said: 'I will show you the root.'

They walked single file away from the homestead down a kaffir path. It was a blazing December afternoon, with the sky full of hot rain-clouds. Everything was hot: the sun was like a bronze tray whirling overhead, there was a heat shimmer over the fields, the soil was scorching underfoot, the dusty wind blew gritty and thick and warm in their faces. It was a terrible day, fit only for reclining on a verandah with iced drinks, which is where they would normally have been at that hour.

From time to time, remembering that on the day of the snake it had taken ten minutes to find the root, someone asked: 'Is it much further, Gideon?' And Gideon would answer over his shoulder, with angry politeness: 'I'm looking for the root, baas.' And indeed, he would frequently bend sideways and trail his hand among the grasses with a gesture that was insulting in its perfunctoriness. He walked them through the bush along unknown paths for two hours, in that melting destroying heat, so that the sweat trickled coldly down them and their heads ached. They were all quite silent: the Farquars because they were angry, the scientist because he was being proved right again; there was no such plant. His was a tactful silence.

At last, six miles from the house, Gideon suddenly decided they had had enough; or perhaps his anger evaporated at that moment. He picked up, without an attempt at looking anything but casual, a handful of blue flowers from the grass, flowers that had been growing plentifully all down the paths they had come.

He handed them to the scientist without looking at him, and

marched off by himself on the way home, leaving them to follow him if they chose.

When they got back to the house, the scientist went to the kitchen to thank Gideon: he was being very polite, even though there was an amused look in his eyes. Gideon was not there. Throwing the flowers casually into the back of his car, the eminent visitor departed on his way back to his laboratory.

Gideon was back in his kitchen in time to prepare dinner, but he was sulking. He spoke to Mrs. Farquar like an unwilling servant. It was days before they liked each other again.

The Farquars made enquiries about the root from their labourers. Sometimes they were answered with distrustful stares. Sometimes the natives said: 'We do not know. We have never heard of the root.' One, the cattle boy, who had been with them a long time, and had grown to trust them a little, said: 'Ask your boy in the kitchen. Now, there's a doctor for you. He's the son of a famous medicine man who used to be in these parts, and there's nothing he cannot cure.' Then he added politely: 'Of course, he's not as good as the white man's doctor, we know that, but he's good for us.'

After some time, when the soreness had gone from between the Farquars and Gideon, they began to joke: 'When are you going to show us the snake-root, Gideon?' And he would laugh and shake his head, saying, a little uncomfortably: 'But I did show you, missus, have you forgotten?'

Much later, Teddy, as a schoolboy, would come into the kitchen and say: 'You old rascal, Gideon! Do you remember that time you tricked us all by making us walk miles all over the veld for nothing? It was so far my father had to carry me!'

And Gideon would double up with polite laughter. After much laughing, he would suddenly straighten himself up, wipe his old eyes, and look sadly at Teddy, who was grinning mischievously at him across the kitchen: 'Ah, Little Yellow Head, how you have grown! Soon you will be grown up with a farm of your own . . . '

DORIS LESSING

Saki

Saki (Hector Hugh Munro) was born in Akyab, Burma in 1870. After the death of their mother, the children were sent to North Devon to live with their grandmother and two fearsome aunts. The upbringing dispensed by these aunts had a marked effect on Saki, and many of the characters and attitudes to be found in his stories can be traced back to this period. In 1893 he took up a post with the Police in Burma but his health could not stand the climate and he was forced to return to England. Here he soon established for himself a reputation as a political satirist and from 1902 to 1908 travelled widely as foreign correspondent for the *Morning Post*, after which he settled in London. When war broke out in 1914, he enlisted immediately in the army. He was twice offered a commission but on both occasions refused it. Shortly before his death on 14 November, 1916, he was promoted to corporal.

Saki was also a novelist and a playright but his reputation rests mainly on his six volumes of short stories, all written between 1904 and 1914. Most of the stories are very short and provide maliciously amusing pictures of the prosperous middle classes in Edwardian England; a number, however, have a more macabre flavour to them. 'The Lumber Room' (*Storytellers 1*) is a comparatively gentle example of the way in which he poked fun at the pompous and hypocritical. 'Sredni Vashtar' (*Storytellers 2*) combines satire with an uncanny grimness. Both the women in these stories were modelled on his own fearsome Aunt Augusta: 'Aunt Augusta was an autocrat and had to be obeyed. She is more or less depicted in 'Sredni Vashtar' but the aunt in 'The Lumber Room' is herself to the life. Both aunts were guilty of mental cruelty and we often longed for revenge . . . '—Saki's stories, many of which have an unexpected twist at the end, are available in a number of anthologies and various omnibus editions.

The Lumber Room

THE children were to be driven, as a special treat, to the sands at Jagborough. Nicholas was not to be of the party; he was in disgrace. Only that morning he had refused to eat his wholesome bread-and-milk on the seemingly frivolous ground that there was a frog in it. Older and wiser and better people had told him that there could not possibly be a frog in his bread-and-milk and that he was not to talk nonsense; he continued, nevertheless, to talk what seemed the veriest nonsense, and described with much detail the coloration and markings of the alleged frog. The dramatic part of the incident was that there really was a frog in Nicholas' basin of bread-and-milk; he had put it there himself, so he felt entitled to know something about it. The sin of taking a frog from the garden and putting it into a bowl of wholesome bread-and-milk was enlarged on at great length, but the fact that stood out clearest in the whole affair, as it presented itself to the mind of Nicholas, was that the older, wiser, and better people had been proved to be profoundly in error in matters about which they had expressed the utmost assurance.

'You said there couldn't possibly be a frog in my bread-and-milk; there *was* a frog in my bread-and-milk,' he repeated, with the insistence of a skilled tactician who does not intend to shift from favourable ground.

So his boy-cousin and girl-cousin and his quite uninteresting younger brother were to be taken to Jagborough sands that afternoon and he was to stay at home. His cousins' aunt, who insisted, by an unwarranted stretch of imagination, in styling herself his aunt also, had hastily invented the Jagborough expedition in order to impress on Nicholas the delights that he had justly forfeited by his disgraceful conduct at the breakfast-table. It was her habit, whenever one of the children fell from grace, to improvise something of a festival nature from which the offender would be rigorously debarred; if all the children sinned collectively they were suddenly informed of a circus in a neighbouring town, a circus of unrivalled merit and uncounted elephants, to which, but for their depravity, they would have been taken that very day.

A few decent tears were looked for on the part of Nicholas when the moment for the departure of the expedition arrived. As a matter of fact, however, all the crying was done by his girl-cousin, who scraped her knee rather painfully against the step of the carriage as she was scrambling in.

'How she did howl,' said Nicholas cheerfully, as the party drove off without any of the elation of high spirits that should have characterised it.

'She'll soon get over that,' said the *soi-disant* aunt; 'it will be a glorious afternoon for racing about over those beautiful sands. How they will enjoy themselves!'

'Bobby won't enjoy himself much, and he won't race much either,' said Nicholas with a grim chuckle; 'his boots are hurting him. They're too tight.'

'Why didn't he tell me they were hurting?' asked the aunt with some asperity.

'He told you twice, but you weren't listening. You often don't listen when we tell you important things.'

'You are not to go into the gooseberry garden,' said the aunt, changing the subject.

'Why not?' demanded Nicholas.

'Because you are in disgrace,' said the aunt loftily.

Nicholas did not admit the flawlessness of the reasoning; he felt perfectly capable of being in disgrace and in a gooseberry garden at the same moment. His face took on an expression of considerable obstinacy. It was clear to his aunt that he was determined to get into the gooseberry garden, 'only,' as she remarked to herself, 'because I have told him he is not to.'

Now the gooseberry garden had two doors by which it might be entered, and once a small person like Nicholas could slip in there he could effectually disappear from view amid the masking growth of artichokes, raspberry canes, and fruit bushes. The aunt had many other things to do that afternoon, but she spent an hour or two in trivial gardening operations among flower beds and shrubberies, whence she could keep a watchful eye on the two doors that led to the forbidden paradise. She was a woman of few ideas, with immense powers of concentration.

Nicholas made one or two sorties into the front garden, wriggling his way with obvious stealth of purpose towards one or other of the doors, but never able for a moment to evade the aunt's watchful eye. As a matter of fact, he had no intention of trying to get into the gooseberry garden, but it was extremely convenient for him that his aunt should believe that he had; it was a belief that would keep her on self-imposed sentry-duty for the greater part of the afternoon. Having thoroughly confirmed and fortified her suspicions, Nicholas slipped back into the house and rapidly put into execution a plan of action that had long germinated in his brain. By standing on a chair in the library one could reach a shelf on which reposed a fat, important-looking key. The key was as important as it looked; it was the instrument which kept the mysteries of the lumber-room secure from unauthorised intrusion which opened a way only for aunts and such-like privileged persons. Nicholas had not had much experience of the art of fitting keys into keyholes and turning locks, but for some days past he had practised with the key of the schoolroom door; he did not believe in trusting too much to luck and accident. The key turned stiffly in the lock, but it turned. The door opened, and Nicholas was in an unknown land, compared with which the gooseberry garden was a stale delight, a mere material pleasure.

Often and often Nicholas had pictured to himself what the lumber-room might be like, that region that was so carefully sealed from youthful eyes and concerning which no questions were ever answered. It came up to his expectations. In the first place it was large and dimly lit, one high window opening on to the forbidden garden being its only source of illumination. In the second place it was a storehouse of unimagined treasures. The aunt-by-assertion was one of those people who think that things spoil by use and consign them to dust and damp by way of preserving them. Such parts of the house as Nicholas knew best were rather bare and cheerless, but here there were wonderful things for the eye to feast on. First and foremost there was a piece of framed tapestry that was evidently meant to be a fire-screen. To Nicholas it was a living, breathing story; he sat down on a roll of Indian hangings, glowing in wonderful colours beneath a layer of dust, and took in all the details of the tapestry picture. A man, dressed in the hunting costume of some remote period, had just transfixed a stag with an arrow; it could not have been a difficult shot because the stag was only one or two paces away from him; in the thickly growing vegetation that the picture suggested it would not have been difficult to creep up to a feeding stag, and the two spotted dogs that were springing forward to join in the chase had evidently been trained to keep to heel till the arrow was discharged. That part of the picture was simple, if interesting, but did the huntsman see, what Nicholas saw, that four galloping wolves were coming in his direction through the wood? There might be more than four of them hidden behind the trees, and in any case would the man and his dogs be able to cope with the four wolves if they made an attack? The man had only two arrows left in his quiver, and he might miss with one or both of them; all one knew about his skill in shooting was that he could hit a large stag at a ridiculously short range. Nicholas sat for many golden minutes revolving the possibilities of the scene; he was inclined to think that there were more than four wolves and that the man and his dogs were in a tight corner.

But there were other objects of delight and interest claiming his instant attention; there were quaint twisted candlesticks in the shape of snakes, and a teapot fashioned like a china duck, out of whose open beak the tea was supposed to come. How dull and shapeless the nursery teapot seemed in comparison! And there was a carved sandal-wood box packed tight with aromatic cotton-wool, and between the layers of cotton-wool were little brass figures, hump-necked bulls, and peacocks and goblins, delightful to see and to handle. Less promising in appearance was a large square book with plain black covers; Nicholas peeped into it, and, behold, it was full of coloured pictures of birds. And such birds! In the garden, and in the lanes when he went for a walk, Nicholas came across a few birds, of which the largest were an occasional magpie or wood-pigeon; here were herons and bustards, kites, toucans, tiger-bitterns, brush turkeys, ibises, golden pheasants, a whole portrait gallery of undreamed-of creatures. And as he was admiring the colouring of the mandarin duck and assigning a life-history to it, the voice of his aunt in shrill vociferation of his name came from the gooseberry garden without. She had grown suspicious of his long disappearance, and had leapt to the conclusion that he had climbed over the wall behind the sheltering screen of the lilac bushes; she was now engaged in energetic and rather hopeless search for him among the artichokes and raspberry canes.

'Nicholas, Nicholas!' she screamed, 'you are to come out of this at once. It's no use trying to hide there; I can see you all the time.'

It was probably the first time for twenty years that anyone had smiled in that lumber-room.

Presently the angry repetitions of Nicholas' name gave way to a shriek, and a cry for somebody to come quickly. Nicholas shut the book, restored it carefully to its place in a corner, and shook some dust from a neighbouring pile of newspapers over it. Then he crept from the room, locked the door, and replaced the key exactly where he had found it. His aunt was still calling his name when he sauntered into the front garden.

'Who's calling?' he asked.

'Me,' came the answer from the other side of the wall; 'didn't you hear me? I've been looking for you in the gooseberry garden, and I've slipped into the rain-water tank. Luckily there's no water in it, but the sides are slippery and I can't get out. Fetch the little ladder from under the cherry tree—'

'I was told I wasn't to go into the gooseberry garden,' said Nicholas promptly.

'I told you not to, and now I tell you that you may,' came the voice from the rain-water tank, rather impatiently.

'Your voice doesn't sound like aunt's,' objected Nicholas; 'you may be the Evil One tempting me to be disobedient. Aunt often tells me that the Evil One tempts me and that I always yield. This time I'm not going to yield.'

'Don't talk nonsense,' said the prisoner in the tank; 'go and fetch the ladder.'

'Will there be strawberry jam for tea?' asked Nicholas innocently.

'Certainly there will be,' said the aunt, privately resolving that Nicholas should have none of it.

'Now I know that you are the Evil One and not aunt,' shouted Nicholas gleefully; 'when we asked aunt for strawberry jam yesterday she said there wasn't any. I know there are four jars of it in the store cupboard, because I looked, and of course you know it's there, but *she* doesn't, because she said there wasn't any. Oh, Devil, you *have* sold yourself!'

There was an unusual sense of luxury in being able to talk to an aunt as though one was talking to the Evil One, but Nicholas knew, with childish discernment, that such luxuries were not to be over-indulged in. He walked noisily away, and it was a kitchen-maid, in search of parsley, who eventually rescued the aunt from the rain-water tank.

Tea that evening was partaken of in a fearsome silence. The tide had been at its highest when the children had arrived at Jagborough Cove, so there had been no sands to play on, a circumstance that the aunt had overlooked in the haste of organising her punitive expedition. The tightness of Bobby's boots had had disastrous effect on his temper the whole of the afternoon, and altogether the children could not have been said to have enjoyed themselves. The aunt maintained the frozen mute-ness of one who has suffered undignified and unmerited detention in a rain-water tank for thirty-five minutes. As for Nicholas, he, too, was silent, in the absorption of one who has much to think about; it was just possible, he considered, that the huntsman would escape with his hounds while the wolves feasted on the stricken stag.

SAKI

35

Stephen Crane

Stephen Crane was born in Newark in the State of New Jersey, U.S.A., on 1 November, 1871. He was the fourteenth child of a clerical family. His father, a Methodist minister, died in 1880, but Stephen's strict upbringing was continued just as rigorously by his mother. He spent a short time at university and then became a newspaper reporter in New York. His first novel, *Maggie: A Girl of the Streets* (1893), was printed at his own expense and was a commercial failure. The next, *The Red Badge of Courage*, appeared initially as a serial in a newspaper and was published as a book the following year, 1895. Like 'A Mystery of Heroism' (*Storytellers 1*), it dealt with the American Civil War. The same basic theme also occurs in both stories: under the stress of battle an ordinary soldier develops, without intending to do so, into a hero—a hero, however, who is real, who knows the meaning of fear, and who realises something of the truth about himself. This concern with the bravery of ordinary men shows itself again in 'The Veteran' (*Storytellers 2*).

The Red Badge of Courage was widely acclaimed and at the age of twenty-four Stephen Crane became a literary celebrity. Although he had, in fact, never been involved in a war when he wrote this novel, he became much sought after as a war correspondent because of the realistic atmosphere he was able to evoke. His experiences as a reporter in the Spanish-American and Graeco-Turkish wars provided him with material for several other books. But the American public, although continuing to admire his stories, came to disapprove of his 'dissolute' way of life. It was perhaps partly to escape their censure that he moved to England, where he spent his last years near Rye in Sussex. He died in the Black Forest in June, 1900.

A Mystery of Heroism

THE dark uniforms of the men were so coated with dust from the incessant wrestling of the two armies that the regiment almost seemed a part of the clay bank which shielded them from the shells. On the top of the hill a battery was arguing in tremendous roars with some other guns, and to the eye of the infantry the artillerymen, the guns, the caissons, the horses, were distinctly outlined upon the blue sky. When a piece was fired, a red streak as round as a log flashed low in the heavens, like a monstrous bolt of lightning. The men of the battery wore white duck trousers, which somehow emphasised their legs; and when they ran and crowded in little groups at the bidding of the shouting officers, it was more impressive than usual to the infantry.

Fred Collins, of A Company, was saying: 'Thunder! I wisht I had a drink. Ain't there any water round here?' Then somebody yelled: 'There goes th' bugler!'

As the eyes of half the regiment swept in one machine-like movement, there was an instant's picture of a horse in a great convulsive leap of a death-wound and a rider leaning back with a crooked arm and spread fingers before his face. On the ground was the crimson terror of an exploding shell, with fibres of flame that seemed like lances. A glittering bugle swung clear of the rider's back as fell headlong the horse and the man. In the air was an odour as from a conflagration.

Sometimes they of the infantry looked down at a fair little meadow which spread at their feet. Its long green grass was rippling gently in a breeze. Beyond it was the grey form of a house half torn to pieces by shells and by the busy axes of soldiers who had pursued firewood. The line of an old fence was now dimly marked by long weeds and by an occasional post. A shell had blown the well-house to fragments. Little lines of grey smoke ribboning upward from some embers indicated the place where had stood the barn.

From beyond a curtain of green woods there came the sound of some stupendous scuffle, as if two animals of the size of islands were fighting. At a distance there were occasional appearances of swift-moving men, horses, batteries, flags, and with the crashing of infantry volleys were heard, often, wild and frenzied cheers. In the midst of it all Smith and Ferguson, two privates of A Company, were engaged in a heated discussion which involved the greatest questions of the national existence.

The battery on the hill presently engaged in a frightful duel. The white legs of the gunners scampered this way and that way, and the officers redoubled their shouts. The guns, with their demeanours of stolidity and courage, were typical of something infinitely self-possessed in this clamour of death that swirled around the hill.

One of a 'swing' team was suddenly smitten quivering to the ground, and his maddened brethren dragged his torn body in their struggle to escape from this turmoil and danger. A young soldier astride one of the leaders swore and fumed in his saddle and furiously jerked at the bridle. An officer screamed out an order so violently that his voice broke and ended the sentence in a falsetto shriek.

The leading company of the infantry regiment was somewhat exposed, and the colonel ordered it moved more fully under the shelter of the hill. There was the clank of steel against steel.

A lieutenant of the battery rode down and passed them, holding his right arm carefully in his left hand. And it was as if this arm was not at all a part of him, but belonged to another man. His sober and reflective charger went slowly. The officer's face was grimy and perspiring, and his uniform was tousled as if he had been in direct grapple with an enemy. He smiled grimly when the men stared at him. He turned his horse towards the meadow.

Collins, of A Company, said: 'I wisht I had a drink. I bet there's water in that there ol' well yonder!'

'Yes; but how you goin' to get it?'

For the little meadow which intervened was now suffering a terrible onslaught of shells. Its green and beautiful calm had vanished utterly. Brown earth was being flung in monstrous handfuls. And there was a massacre of the young blades of grass. They were being torn, burned, obliterated. Some curious fortune of the battle had made this gentle little meadow the object of the

red hate of the shells, and each one as it exploded seemed like an imprecation in the face of a maiden.

The wounded officer who was riding across this expanse said to himself: 'Why, they couldn't shoot any harder if the whole army was massed here!'

A shell struck the grey ruins of the house, and as, after the roar, the shattered wall fell in fragments, there was a noise which resembled the flapping of shutters during a wild gale of winter. Indeed, the infantry paused in the shelter of the bank appeared as men standing upon a shore contemplating a madness of the sea. The angel of calamity had under its glance the battery upon the hill. Fewer white-legged men laboured about the guns. A shell had smitten one of the pieces, and after the flare, the smoke, the dust, the wrath of this blow were gone, it was possible to see white legs stretched horizontally upon the ground. And at that interval to the rear where it is the business of battery horses to stand with their noses to the fight, awaiting the command to drag their guns out of the destruction, or into it, or wheresoever these incomprehensible humans demanded with whip and spur—in this line of passive and dumb spectators, whose fluttering hearts yet would not let them forget the iron laws of man's control of them—in this rank of brute-soldiers there had been relentless and hideous carnage. From the ruck of bleeding and prostrate horses, the men of the infantry could see one animal raising its stricken body with its forelegs and turning its nose with mystic and profound eloquence toward the sky.

Some comrades joked Collins about his thirst. 'Well, if yeh want a drink so bad, why don't yeh go git it?'

'Well, I will in a minnet, if yeh don't shut up!'

A lieutenant of artillery floundered his horse straight down the hill with as little concern as if it were level ground. As he galloped past the colonel of the infantry, he threw up his hand in swift salute. 'We've got to get out of that,' he roared angrily. He was a

black-bearded officer, and his eyes, which resembled beads, sparkled like those of an insane man. His jumping horse sped along the column of infantry.

The fat major, standing carelessly with his sword held horizontally behind him and with his legs far apart, looked after the receding horseman and laughed. 'He wants to get back with orders pretty quick, or there'll be no batt'ry left,' he observed.

The wise young captain of the second company hazarded to the lieutenant-colonel that the enemy's infantry would probably soon attack the hill, and the lieutenant-colonel snubbed him.

A private in one of the rear companies looked out over the meadow, and then turned to a companion and said, 'Look there, Jim!' It was the wounded officer from the battery, who some time before had started to ride across the meadow, supporting his right arm carefully with his left hand. This man had encountered a shell, apparently, at a time when no one perceived him, and he could now be seen lying face downward with a stirruped foot stretched across the body of his dead horse. A leg of the charger extended slantingly upward, precisely as stiff as a stake. Around this motionless pair the shells still howled.

There was a quarrel in A Company. Collins was shaking his fist in the faces of some laughing comrades. 'Darn yeh! I ain't afraid t' go. If yeh say much, I will go!'

'Of course yeh will! You'll run through that there medder, won't yeh?'

Collins said, in a terrible voice: 'You see now!'

At this ominous threat his comrades broke into renewed jeers.

Collins gave them a dark scowl, and went to find his captain. The latter was conversing with the colonel of the regiment.

'Captain,' said Collins, saluting and standing at attention—in those days all trousers bagged at the knees—'Captain, I want t' get permission to go git some water from that there well over yonder!'

The colonel and the captain swung about simultaneously and stared across the meadow. The captain laughed. 'You must be pretty thirsty, Collins.'

'Yes, sir, I am.'

'Well—ah,' said the captain. After a moment, he asked, 'Can't you wait?'

'No, sir.'

The colonel was watching Collin's face. 'Look here, my lad,' he said, in a pious sort of voice—'Look here, my lad'—Collins was not a lad—'don't you think that's taking pretty big risks for a little drink of water?'

'I dunno,' said Collins uncomfortably. Some of the resentment towards his companions, which perhaps had forced him into this affair, was beginning to fade. 'I dunno w'ether 'tis.'

The colonel and the captain contemplated him for a time.

'Well,' said the captain finally.

'Well,' said the colonel, 'if you want to go, why, go.'

Collins saluted. 'Much obliged t' yeh.'

As he moved away the colonel called after him. 'Take some of the other boys' canteens with you, an' hurry back, now.'

'Yes, sir, I will.'

The colonel and the captain looked at each other then, for it had suddenly occurred that they could not for the life of them tell whether Collins wanted to go or whether he did not.

They turned to regard Collins, and as they perceived him surrounded by gesticulating comrades, the colonel said: 'Well, by thunder! I guess he's going.'

Collins appeared as a man dreaming. In the midst of the questions, the advice, the warnings, all the excited talk of his company mates, he maintained a curious silence.

They were very busy in preparing him for his ordeal. When they inspected him carefully, it was somewhat like the examination that grooms give a horse before a race; and they were amazed, staggered, by the whole affair. Their astonishment found vent in strange repetitions.

'Are yeh sure a-goin' ?' they demanded again and again.

'Certainly I am,' cried Collins at last, furiously.

He strode sullenly away from them. He was swinging five or six canteens by their cords. It seemed that his cap would not remain firmly on his head, and often he reached and pulled it down over his brow.

There was a general movement in the compact column. The long animal-like thing moved slightly. Its four hundred eyes were turned upon the figure of Collins.

'Well, sir, if that ain't th' derndest thing! I never thought Fred Collins had the blood in him for that kind of business.'

'What's he goin' to do, anyhow ?'

'He's goin' to that well there after water.'

'We ain't dyin' of thirst, are we ? That's foolishness.'

'Well, somebody put him up to it, an' he's doin' it.'

'Say, he must be a desperate cuss.'

When Collins faced the meadow and walked away from the regiment, he was vaguely conscious that a chasm, the deep valley of all prides, was suddenly between him and his comrades. It was provisional, but the provision was that he return as a victor. He had blindly been led by quaint emotions, and laid himself under an obligation to walk squarely up to the face of death.

But he was not sure that he wished to make a retraction, even if he could do so without shame. As a matter of truth, he was sure of very little. He was mainly surprised.

It seemed to him supernaturally strange that he had allowed his mind to manoeuvre his body into such a situation. He understood that it might be called dramatically great.

However, he had no full appreciation of anything, excepting that he was actually conscious of being dazed. He could feel his dulled mind groping after the form and colour of this incident. He wondered why he did not feel some keen agony of fear cutting his sense like a knife. He wondered at this, because human expression had said loudly for centuries that men should feel afraid of certain things, and that all men who did not feel this fear were phenomena-heroes.

He was, then, a hero. He suffered that disappointment which we would all have if we discovered that we were ourselves capable of those deeds which we most admire in history and legend. This, then, was a hero. After all, heroes were not much.

No, it could not be true. He was not a hero. Heroes had no shames in their lives, and, as for him, he remembered borrowing fifteen dollars from a friend and promising to pay it back the next day, and then avoiding that friend for ten months. When, at home, his mother had aroused him for the early labour of his life on the farm, it had often been his fashion to be irritable, childish, diabolical; and his mother had died since he had come to the war.

44

He saw that, in this matter of the well, the canteens, the shells, he was an intruder in the land of fine deeds.

He was now about thirty paces from his comrades. The regiment had just turned its many faces toward him.

From the forest of terrific noises there suddenly emerged a little uneven line of men. They fired fiercely and rapidly at distant foliage on which appeared little puffs of white smoke. The spatter of skirmish firing was added to the thunder of the guns on the hill. The little line of men ran forward. A colour-sergeant fell flat with his flag as if he had slipped on ice. There was hoarse cheering from this distant field.

Collins suddenly felt that two demon fingers were pressed into his ears. He could see nothing but flying arrows, flaming red. He lurched from the shock of this explosion, but he made a mad rush for the house, which he viewed as a man submerged to the neck in a boiling surf might view the shore. In the air little pieces of shell

howled, and the earthquake explosions drove him insane with the menace of their roar. As he ran the canteens knocked together with a rhythmical tinkling.

As he neared the house, each detail of the scene became vivid to him. He was aware of some bricks of the vanished chimney lying on the sod. There was a door which hung by one hinge.

Rifle bullets called forth by the insistent skirmishers came from the far-off bank of foliage. They mingled with the shells and the pieces of shells until the air was torn in all directions by hootings, yells, howls. The sky was full of fiends who directed all their wild rage at his head.

When he came to the well, he flung himself face downward and peered into its darkness. There were furtive silver glintings some feet from the surface. He grabbed one of the canteens and, unfastening its cap, swung it down by the cord. The water flowed slowly in with an indolent gurgle.

And now, as he lay with his face turned away, he was suddenly smitten with the terror. It came upon his heart like the grasp of claws. All the power faded from his muscles. For an instant he was no more than a dead man.

The canteen filled with a maddening slowness, in the manner of all bottles. Presently he recovered his strength and addressed a screaming oath to it. He leaned over until it seemed as if he intended to try to push water into it with his hands. His eyes as he gazed down into the well shone like two pieces of metal, and in their expression was a great appeal and a great curse. The stupid water derided him.

There was the blaring thunder of a shell. Crimson light shone through the swift-boiling smoke and made a pink reflection on part of the wall of the well. Collins jerked out his arm and canteen with the same motion that a man would use in withdrawing his head from a furnace.

He scrambled erect and glared and hesitated. On the ground near him lay the old well bucket, with a length of rusty chain. He lowered it swiftly into the well. The bucket struck the water and then, turning lazily over, sank. When, with hand reaching tremblingly over hand, he hauled it out, it knocked often against the walls of the well and spilled some of its contents.

In running with a filled bucket, a man can adopt but one kind of gait. So, through this terrible field over which screamed practical angels of death, Collins ran in the manner of a farmer chased out of a dairy by a bull.

His face went staring white with anticipation—anticipation of a blow that would whirl him around and down. He would fall as he had seen other men fall, the life knocked out of them so suddenly that their knees were no more quick to touch the ground than their heads. He saw the long blue line of the regiment but his comrades were standing looking at him from the edge of an impossible star. He was aware of some deep wheel-ruts and hoofprints in the sod beneath his feet.

The artillery officer who had fallen in this meadow had been making groans in the teeth of the tempest of sound. These futile cries, wrenched from him by his agony, were heard only by shells, bullets. When wild-eyed Collins came running, this officer raised himself. His face contorted and blanched from pain, he was about to utter some great beseeching cry. But suddenly his face straightened, and he called: 'Say, young man, give me a drink of water, will you?'

Collins had no room amid his emotions for surprise. He was mad from the threats of destruction.

'I can't!' he screamed, and in his reply was a full description of his quaking apprehension. His cap was gone and his hair was riotous. His clothes made it appear that he had been dragged over the ground by the heels. He ran on.

The officer's head sank down, and one elbow crooked. His foot in its brass-bound stirrup still stretched over the body of his horse, and the other leg was under the steed.

But Collins turned. He came dashing back. His face had now turned grey, and in his eyes was all terror. 'Here it is! Here it is!'

The officer was as a man gone in drink. His arm bent like a twig. His head drooped as if his neck were of willow. He was sinking to the ground, to lie face downward.

Collins grabbed him by the shoulder. 'Here it is. Here's your drink. Turn over. Turn over, man, for God's sake!'

With Collins hauling at his shoulder, the officer twisted his body and fell with his face turned toward that region where lived the unspeakable noises of the swirling missiles. There was the faintest shadow of a smile on his lips as he looked at Collins. He gave a sigh, a little primitive breath like that from a child.

Collins tried to hold the bucket steadily, but his shaking hands caused the water to splash all over the face of the dying man. Then he jerked it away and ran on.

The regiment gave him a welcoming roar. The grimed faces were wrinkled in laughter.

His captain waved the bucket away. 'Give it to the men!'

The two genial, skylarking lieutenants were the first to gain possession of it. They played over it in their fashion.

When one tried to drink, the other teasingly knocked his elbow. 'Don't, Billie! You'll make me spill it,' said the one. The other laughed.

Suddenly there was an oath, the thud of wood on the ground, and a swift murmur of astonishment among the ranks. The two lieutenants glared at each other. The bucket lay on the ground, empty.

STEPHEN CRANE

49

Judith Wright

Judith Wright (Mrs. J. McKinney) was born in Australia, near Armidale, New South Wales, in 1915. She spent much of her early girlhood in the outback and, because there were no schools nearby, received her first education through the N.S.W. Correspondence School. Then, after attending the New England Girls' School, she went to Sydney University. This was followed by a year in Europe. When she returned to Australia, she worked as a stenographer, a secretary, a statistician and an agriculturalist. She now lives with her husband at Mount Tamborine in Southern Queensland.

She is best known for her poetry, being recognised as one of the most outstanding poets writing in English today, and certainly Australia's leading contributor. Her first book of poems, *The Moving Image*, was published in 1946; since then she has written several more and has also edited *The Oxford Book of Australian Verse*. Her short stories, however, are not written in what is commonly thought of as a 'poetic' style: there are no involved descriptions or exaggerated images; instead the prose is clear and economic. Her poet's understanding is revealed more by her deep feeling for Australian life, both in the suburbs and in the country, as shown by 'In the Park' (*Storytellers 1*) and 'The Rabbiter' (*Storytellers 2*) respectively. Her dialogue, for example, has an authentic Australian tone, without relying on a multitude of idioms to create the effect. She has published only one volume of short stories, *The Nature of Love* (1966). Her other work includes literary criticism, four books for children and a biographical novel.

In the Park

VIVI's mother was taking her to the Park to see the flowers and the birds in cages. Vivi had been to the Park before; but it was a long way, right to the other side of town in the bus, and it was a long time ago. She remembered the bus but not the birds; she remembered the lake and that she mustn't get her feet wet.

Her mother put Vivi's new white sandals on for her, and tied a blue bow in her hair. Outside the summer was shrilling like the noise in the sawmill down the road; the day was so hot that Gran lay in her cane long-chair and fanned herself.

'Why you should want to take the poor child to the Park on a day like this I can't see. That long hot ride in the bus! But you get these notions in your head, and I know very well it wouldn't matter what I said, I can't talk you out of it.'

'There'll be a cool breeze out there; and she needs a bit of a change now and then. Our room isn't all that nice for a kid on a day like this, with the sun coming straight in like it does; and you don't like her messing up the rest of the house. I'd rather not see her playing in the street with those little Gardners all the time.'

Her mother called Gran sometimes Gran and sometimes Mrs. Coleman. Today she had been calling her Mrs. Coleman; it was something about the breakfast washing-up. Those days their voices made Vivi wince when they spoke to oné another, as though she had tasted one of the little green mangoes that plumped on the grass in the garden.

Gran closed up her mouth, the little brown hairs around it bright with tiny drops from the heat; then she looked at Vivi and smiled, and tapped her leg with the fan. 'Anyway, Vivi, you look nice in those new shoes. Here's threepence for lollies.'

Vivi sat on the bus seat, her legs uncomfortable. She couldn't lean back unless her legs stuck straight out in front of her, and if she sat on the edge of the seat, she fell off when the bus turned a corner. She tried it, and slid sideways and clutched at her mother. Her mother brushed her hand away with an annoyed sound.

'Stop it, can't you? You'll crush my dress.'

Vivi looked humbly at the dress; it was new, with red flowers. She looked at her mother's red hat that made her face look like a stranger's, like a powdered flower in the red light that shone through the hat and seemed to make a separate coloured world in which her mother lived. Her mother's face was special like that and strange, because of the Park, Vivi thought; because she hardly ever went to the Park and now she was going. But the bus bounced so much that Vivi had to hold on with both hands to the seat in front. She began to think about her threepence, lying in her mother's handbag across her knees.

Now there were trees, a whole avenue of trees with leaves like green feathers. 'This is the road to the Park,' her mother said; and she took a mirror from her handbag and powdered her face again. Vivi craned to look too, but her mother snapped the mirror back into the case.

There was a turnstile; there was a little kiosk that sold chewing-gum and soft drinks.

'Gran gave me threepence,' said Vivi, hanging back on her mother's hand.

'Oh, come *on*, Vivi.'

'Gran give me threepence to buy lollies.' Vivi's voice went high, the way it did when she was ready to cry. Her mother took her back to the kiosk, walking quickly, and Vivi bought some toffees.

'Now, will you come on?' Her mother set off down a long path with flowers on each side, and Vivi followed, taking the paper off a toffee.

There was a terrible cry, a dry wooden shriek. Vivi stood still with shock. A huge white bird clung to the wires of a cage beside the path; he lifted his yellow hair at her and leaned against the wire with one claw out.

'Mum! Mum!' cried Vivi.

'What is it now?'

'Come back, I'm frightened.'

'Oh, don't be silly, Vivi. It's only a cockatoo.'

Knowing the bird's name made it seem quite different. 'It's only a cockatoo,' Vivi repeated aloud, and at once the bird shrank and became nothing but a cockatoo. She threw the toffee-paper at it.

'Come *on*, Vivi.' Her mother was far down the path.

Vivi ran and caught her mother's hand. It was cold, it swung hers to and fro, jerkily. Vivi looked up, surprised. There was a man walking down the path towards them. Vivi had seen him before, when she was in the town with her mother, and he had stopped to talk; but this time her mother's hand said he was important.

'Well, Vera. So you did come?'

'Thought the Park might be cool today. It's too hot in the house.'

'I didn't know I'd invited both of you. Couldn't we have a talk by ourselves, for once?'

'What makes you think I came to meet you, anyway? I'm giving the kid an outing. She's my kid, isn't she?'

And she shook Vivi's arm. 'Say hullo to Mr. Malley.'

'Hullo,' said Vivi. But she had remembered something else about the Park. 'You're not my Da,' she said.

The man laughed, but he sounded angry. 'Not your Da? Of course I'm not. What's the idea?'

Her mother shook her arm again. 'We came here once before with Don. I s'pose she remembered. That was the last time he was here.'

'How long ago's that?'

'Eighteen months.'

'It's a wonder she remembers him at all. You haven't heard from him?'

'He don't write to his mother, either. But he'll be back.'

'This year, next year, eh?' Mr. Malley bent down to Vivi. 'Here's sixpence. You run off and get yourself something at the shop.'

But Vivi drew back. She knew about not taking money from strange men. 'My Gran give me threepence. I've got some lollies.'

And her mother swung her hand again. 'Vivi can stick around; I want to keep an eye on her. If you don't like having her about, there's no need to stay, see? I told you, it wasn't to meet you I came'.

'Okay, okay.' Mr. Malley had a sideways smile. 'You came all off your own bat and I never said a word. Come on, now, be your age. Let's all sit down on a seat somewhere and have a nice family chat.'

'Well.' Her mother still held her hand. 'I s'pose we could do that for a little while. I promised her I'd show her the birds.'

'Afterwards, afterwards.' Mr. Malley moved them down the path. There was a seat under a palm-tree, and her mother pulled Vivi down to sit between the two of them.

The lake was down there, but Vivi wanted to see the birds. There was an emu, Gran had said, and something else. She peeled herself another toffee and waited.

But they took no notice of her, and her legs hanging down from the seat grew restless. She drummed her feet against the bar under the bench. Her mother shook her shoulder again. 'Don't do that, Vivi.'

She began to wriggle with discomfort. No one looked at her. She took out another toffee and after a while put it on the man's knee. He went on talking.

'Look, mister,' she said. 'Look what I gave you.'

Mr. Malley picked it up, still talking, and put it in his pocket. He did not say 'Thank you,' and she began to regret the toffee. She sighed and wriggled again. A girl ran by with a hoop.

'Can I get down, Mum? Mum, can I get down?'

'Oh, stop whining, Vivi. Go and play, then.'

She slid down and spilt the toffees out of the bag. There were ants running about on the bare ground in front of the seat. She crouched down to pick up the toffees.

'Mum! An ant bit me!'

55

'Oh, Vivienne! Give us a bit of peace, can't you? Here, take the bag and run away.'

At this the ant-bite, which had not really hurt her, began to sting. Vivi put her finger in her mouth to stop the tears. Red in the face, she stamped her foot and moved away. She stopped to look back after a minute, but her mother did not turn.

Some grey birds flew overhead and circled round with a whirring noise, before they settled on the grass. Were these the birds she had come to see? Vivi stamped at them, and they lifted into the air and fell again. She began to walk after them, stalking them. Their feathers shone in the sun with changing colours as they walked about, cooing. Their round red eyes peering at her, staring and remote; their necks thrust to and fro like Gran's when she was in a temper. Vivi would have liked to catch one and pull out its feathers, but they kept moving farther away, and when she stretched out her hand they rose out of her reach into the air.

Now a beetle scrambled past her through the grass. She followed it slowly and dared at last to put out a finger and touch it as it climbed a grass-stem. At once it put out four whizzing arms and flew away.

She stood and listened. There were strange noises up the path —twitterings and cries and squeaking sounds. She could see more cages there, like the one with the cockatoo. She began to walk towards them, stopping and stamping down any stems of grass that stood higher than the rest, until they lay flat.

A little boy stood watching her; he had a white shirt and a pink ice cream cone. He took a lick from the cone and stared over it.

Vivi began to sing loudly. 'Who's afraid of the big bad wolf?' she sang; the little Gardners had a gramophone that sang that tune, and Vivi had learned it. She swaggered, stamping down the grass.

'That grass belongs to my Daddy,' said the little boy. 'Everything here belongs to my Daddy. He's a policeman.'

'You go away,' said Vivi.

'Go away yourself,' said the boy.

Vivi kicked at the grass again, and ran away. The cages were quite near, and people walked up and down and stared into them, but to reach them she had to pass a whole family of people who had spread a rug beside the path and were drinking coloured drinks from bottles and eating potato-flakes from bags. There were two girls bigger than Helen Gardner, and a girl smaller than Vivi, and two grown-ups. A brown puppy played round them.

Vivi stood still, not sure whether to go on. She felt as though she had come a long way, and when she looked back she could not see the seat where her mother was.

The puppy came running. It pranced and crouched in front of her and panted with its tongue out. Vivi knew its name; she had heard one of the girls calling it. 'Micky,' she said, asserting power

over it with the name; but she backed further as the puppy followed. Her heel caught in the grass, and she sat down. The puppy scrambled over her legs and licked her face; it felt warm and friendly. She patted its ear and put her arms round it; they rolled together in the grass.

'Micky,' one of the girls called. 'Micky, come here.' The puppy ran away, and the three girls seized him and rolled him about on the rug, and fed him with potato-flakes. Vivi stood watching for a while, her finger in her mouth, but he did not come back.

Slowly she went on towards the bird-cages, making a wide circle round the rug where the puppy played. The girls did not look at her.

The first cage was bright with movement and gave out a thin shrieking noise. Closer, she saw a crowd of small birds that darted up and down, swung on swings, or clung to the wires of the cage with feet thinner than string. Vivi clung to the wires too, opening and shutting her mouth, licking the iron cross-bars that tasted cold and strange. The birds made a criss-cross of colours in the air, and she stayed there for a long time.

At last she uncurled her fingers and stepped back. 'Cockatoos,' she said, and dragging her hand against the wires she went on.

There were grey stones, there was water running, a pink and white bird shrieked at her and she stamped at it. People kept passing. She had forgotten to look back for her mother.

Now she was at the last cage of all. Something stood there quite close to the wires, tall and grey on long thin legs. Vivi drew back.

It was taller than she was. Was it a bird, was it a person? She spoke to it, but it did not answer. 'Cockatoo,' she said, but she felt it was not the right word.

The bird or person made a step towards her, its face was red, its eyes were large and round. Vivi put her finger in her mouth and looked back at it.

The creature walked towards her and stretched out a great grey arm. Vivi jumped back and stared. Then she took out another toffee and held it towards the red face.

A long beak came towards the wires and Vivi dropped the toffee just inside the cage. The beak picked it up, but dropped it, and came back towards the wires again. Vivi had no words to master it.

Now the creature spread out both arms with a frightening sudden rush of feathers, sending Vivi backwards again, and curved its neck and lifted its feet high, one after the other. It stalked backwards and forwards, it raised its thin legs high in the air with those great grey arms spread wide, it peered at Vivi and stretched its long neck towards her. She watched it, breathing fast. What was it doing? What did it want? It stared and bowed and beckoned, danced and waved its arms. It wanted something.

Vivi began obediently to move her feet as it did, to spread out her arms and bend her head. The bird took a little bobbing run to one side; so did Vivi. It turned its back and ran to the other side of the cage, turned again and ran back, and Vivi met it at the wires, balancing with her arms outstretched. She had forgotten about words; she was intent. She thought of nothing except the movements. When the bird bent, scraped with its foot, jumped in the air, so did she. Her arms were grey and wide, her neck was long, her head posed and bowed.

It shocked her suddenly to hear, as she met the bird again with outstretched arms, a shout of laughter behind her. The bird ran away and Vivi turned. People were watching and laughing. She put her finger in her mouth and for some reason began to cry.

Someone came pushing through the crowd and caught her hand. It was her mother.

'Oh, you bad girl! Running away like that. I thought you'd fallen in the lake.' Her mother wiped her eyes clean with a hand-kerchief. 'And here you are, making a show of yourself. Look at you—sticky toffee all over your face and hands.' She dragged Vivi down the path, and scrubbed her with the wet handkerchief at the drinking fountain.

Then they were going back again up the path, towards the waiting bus. Her mother's fingers hurt her hand; and something else was wrong too. She had lost her bag; there was still a toffee in it.

'I had a toffee left,' she sobbed. 'My bag's gone.'

'Just as well, too. You've had more than enough.'

'I give that man a toffee and he never said thank you. He took it and he never et it.'

Her mother did not answer.

'You ask him to give it back.'

Her mother halted and pulled Vivi round to face her. 'You get this straight right now, Vivi. We're going home. No more toffees, do you hear?'

Vivi dropped her head. She did not cry loudly, but her breath came in gasps and sobs. She scrambled up behind her mother into the empty bus.

Her mother went right to the back, to the very last seat, and put Vivi next to the window and sat beside her. Vivi was still sobbing. She ached with emptiness and she would have liked to lie down on her mother's lap, but her mother was angry with her.

After a while a few more people got in; then her mother moved and took her hand again. 'Tired, Vivi? You can put your head down if you want to.'

Vivi slipped down mutely and gave a long sigh. The tears were drying on her face in a stiff crust. Her mother took off her bonnet, and settled her more comfortably.

'Tell me, what did you go and run away for?'

'I never,' Vivi said. Crying had exhausted her; her voice was nearly asleep. 'Where's the man?' she asked at last.

'Gone away,' her mother said. She spoke in the same quiet

voice that Vivi had used, as though she were tired.

'What for?'

'Cause I told him to. I had to look for you, see, and he didn't want me to.'

'I was glad when you came,' Vivi said. 'He never said thank you and he took my toffee.'

'You forget about him. He's gone now.'

'Will he be here if we come back again? Will he have my toffee?'

'I told you, he's gone. You just shut up about him, see?'

'I'll tell Gran he never said thank you.'

'Don't you tell Gran anything about it, Vivi. Gran don't want to hear about him. You forget him.'

Vivi slid down further, luxuriously, into her mother's lap. 'That big thing,' she said. 'Why did it run about? What did it want?'

'That was a bird. That was a brolga. He was just dancing, the way they do. I suppose he thought you were another brolga.'

'Brolga,' said Vivi. 'I'll tell Gran I want that brolga.'

Her mother said nothing. The bus was full and now it began to move off. She held Vivi on her lap and put the bonnet over her eyes to keep off the sun. Vivi went to sleep.   JUDITH WRIGHT

Jack London

Jack London was born in America in San Francisco in 1876. He came from a poor working class family and was largely self-educated. Before becoming a writer, he was a sailor, gold miner and hobo. In the early 1900s he came to be regarded as 'the popular historian of the Klondike' and even today he is still remembered mainly for such stories as *The Call of the Wild* and *White Fang*—two vividly told tales of animal life in the Frozen North. Much of his work, however, expressed his strong socialist beliefs: *The Iron Heel*, a grimly prophetic novel about the future of civilisation, is perhaps the best known example of this aspect of his work. In virtually all his writing—whether it was about men or animals, set in Alaska or the South Seas, providing an exciting narrative or grim social criticism—there was a savage, brutal streak, an obsession with survival and destruction. This can be seen in both 'Bâtard' (*Storytellers 1*) and 'Love of Life' (*Storytellers 2*).

London, himself, seemed strangely bent on self-destruction. Although he earned as much as $75,000 a year, his financial affairs were invariably in chaos. He spent his money recklessly—on a lavish ranch in California, on an ill-fated world cruise in his own yacht, on a new castle called 'Wolf House' which burned to the ground six weeks before completion. Disillusioned with life, he began drinking heavily, although he continued to produce as many as four books a year in his desperate attempts to make even more money. He died, sick in body and mind, in November, 1916.

Bâtard

BÂTARD was a devil. This was recognised throughout the Northland. 'Hell's Spawn' he was called by many men, but his master, Black Leclère, chose for him the shameful name 'Bâtard'. Now Black Leclère was also a devil, and the twain were well matched. There is a saying that when two devils come together, hell is to pay. This is to be expected, and this certainly was to be expected when Bâtard and Black Leclère came together. The first time they met, Bâtard was a part-grown puppy, lean and hungry, with bitter eyes; and they met with snap and snarl, and wicked looks, for Leclère's upper lip had a wolfish way of lifting and showing the white cruel teeth. And it lifted then, and his eyes glinted viciously, as he reached for Bâtard and dragged him out from the squirming litter. It was certain that they divined each other, for on the instant, Bâtard had buried his puppy fangs in Leclère's hand, and Leclère, with thumb and finger, was coolly choking his young life out of him.

'Sacredam', the Frenchman said softly, flirting the quick blood from his bitten hand and gazing down on the little puppy choking and gasping in the snow.

Leclère turned to John Hamlin, storekeeper of the Sixty Mile Post. 'Dat f' w'at Ah lak heem. 'Ow moch, eh, you, *M'sieu*? 'Ow moch? Ah buy heem, now; Ah buy heem queek.'

And because he hated him with an exceeding bitter hate, Leclère bought Bâtard and gave him his shameful name. And for five years the twain adventured across the Northland, from St. Michael's and the Yukon delta to the head-reaches of the Pelly and even so far as the Peace River, Athabasca, and the Great Slave. And they acquired a reputation for uncompromising wickedness, the like of which never before attached himself to man and dog.

Bâtard did not know his father—hence his name—but, as John Hamlin knew, his father was a great grey timber wolf. But the mother of Bâtard, as he dimly remembered her, was snarling, bickering, obscene, husky, full-fronted and heavy-chested, with a malign eye, a cat-like grip on life, and a genius for trickery and evil. There was neither faith nor trust in her. Her treachery alone could be relied upon, and her wild-wood amours attested her general depravity. Much of evil and much of strength were there in these, Bâtard's progenitors, and, bone and flesh of their bone and flesh, he had inherited it all. And then came Black Leclère, to lay his heavy hand on a bit of pulsating puppy life, to press and prod and mold till it became a big bristling beast, acute in knavery, overspilling with hate, sinister, malignant, diabolical. With a proper master Bâtard might have made an ordinary, fairly efficient sled-dog. He never got the chance: Leclère but confirmed him in his congenital iniquity.

The history of Bâtard and Leclère is a history of war—of five cruel, relentless years, of which their first meeting is fit summary. To begin with, it was Leclère's fault, for he hated with understanding and intelligence, while the long-legged, ungainly puppy hated only blindly, instinctively, without reason or method. At first there were no refinements of cruelty (these were to come later), but simple beatings and crude brutalities. In one of these Bâtard had an ear injured. He never regained control of the riven muscles, and ever after the ear drooped limply down to keep keen the memory of his tormentor. And he never forgot.

His puppyhood was a period of foolish rebellion. He was

always worsted, but he fought back because it was his nature to fight back. And he was unconquerable. Yelping shrilly from the pain of lash and club, he none the less contrived always to throw in the defiant snarl, the bitter vindictive menace of his soul which fetched without fail more blows and beatings. But his was his mother's tenacious grip on life. Nothing could kill him. He flourished under misfortune, grew fat with famine, and out of his terrible struggle for life developed a preternatural intelligence. His were the stealth and cunning of the husky, his mother, and the fierceness and valor of the wolf, his father.

Possibly it was because of his father that he never wailed. His puppy yelps passed with his lanky legs, so that he became grim and taciturn, quick to strike, slow to warn. He answered curse with snarl, and blow with snap, grinning the while his implacable hatred; but never again, under the extremist agony, did Leclère bring from him the cry of fear nor of pain. This unconquerableness but fanned Leclère's wrath and stirred him to greater deviltries.

Did Leclère give Bâtard half a fish and to his mates whole ones, Bâtard went forth to rob other dogs of their fish. Also he robbed caches and expressed himself in a thousand rogueries, till he became a terror to all dogs and masters of dogs. Did Leclère beat Bâtard and fondle Babette—Babette who was not half the worker he was—why Bâtard threw her down in the snow and broke her hind leg in his heavy jaws so that Leclère was forced to shoot her. Likewise, in bloody battles, Bâtard mastered all his team-mates, set them the law of trail and forage, and made them live to the law he set.

In five years he heard but one kind word, received but one soft stroke of a hand, and then he did not know what manner of things they were. He leaped like the untamed thing he was, and his jaws were together in a flash. It was the missionary at Sunrise, a newcomer in the country, who spoke the kind word and gave the soft stroke of the hand. And for six months after, he wrote no letters home to the States, and the surgeon at McQuestion travelled two hundred miles on the ice to save him from blood-poisoning.

Men and dogs looked askance at Bâtard when he drifted into their camps and posts. The men greeted him with feet threateningly lifted for the kick, the dogs with bristling manes and bared fangs. Once a man did kick Bâtard, and Bâtard, with quick wolf snap, closed his jaws like a steel trap on the man's calf and crunched down to the bone. Whereat the man was determined to have his life, only Black Leclère, with ominous eyes and naked hunting-knife, stepped in between. The killing of Bâtard—ah, *sacredam, that* was a pleasure Leclère reserved for himself. Some day it would happen, or else—bah! who was to know? Anyway, the problem would be solved.

For they had become problems to each other. The very breath each drew was a challenge and a menace to the other. Their hate bound them together as love could never bind. Leclère was bent on the coming of the day when Bâtard should wilt in spirit and cringe and whimper at his feet. And Bâtard—Leclère knew what was in Bâtard's mind, and more than once had read it in Bâtard's eyes. And so clearly had he read, that when Bâtard was at his back, he made it a point to glance often over his shoulder.

Men marvelled when Leclère refused large money for the dog. 'Some day you'll kill him and be out his price,' said John Hamlin once, when Bâtard lay panting in the snow where Leclère had kicked him, and no one knew whether his ribs were broken, and no one dared look to see.

'Dat,' said Leclère, dryly, 'dat is my biz'ness, *M'sieu*'.'

And the men marvelled that Bâtard did not run away. They did not understand. But Leclère understood. He was a man who lived much in the open, beyond the sound of human tongue, and he had learned the voices of wind and storm, the sigh of night, the

whisper of dawn, the clash of day. In a dim way he could hear the green things growing, the running of the sap, the bursting of the bud. And he knew the subtle speech of the things that moved, of the rabbit in the snare, the moody raven beating the air with hollow wing, the bald-face shuffling under the moon, the wolf like a grey shadow gliding betwixt the twilight and the dark. And to him Bâtard spoke clear and direct. Full well he understood why Bâtard did not run away, and he looked more often over his shoulder.

When in anger, Bâtard was not nice to look upon, and more than once had he leapt for Leclère's throat, to be stretched quivering and senseless in the snow, by the butt of the ever ready dog-whip. And so Bâtard learned to bide his time. When he reached his full strength and prime of youth, he thought the time had come. He was broad-chested, powerfully muscled, of far more than ordinary size, and his neck from head to shoulders was a mass of bristling hair—to all appearances a full-blooded wolf. Leclère was lying asleep in his furs when Bâtard deemed the time to be ripe. He crept upon him stealthily, head low to earth and lone ear laid back, with a feline softness of tread. Bâtard breathed gently, very gently, and not till he was close at hand did he raise his head. He paused for a moment, and looked at the bronzed bull throat, naked and knotty, and swelling to a deep and steady pulse. The slaver dripped down his fangs and slid off his tongue at the sight, and in that moment he remembered his drooping ear, his un-counted blows and prodigous wrongs, and without a sound sprang on the sleeping man.

Leclère awoke to the pang of the fangs in his throat, and, perfect animal that he was, he awoke clear-headed and with full comprehension. He closed on Bâtard's windpipe with both his hands, and rolled out of his furs to get his weight uppermost. But the thousands of Bâtard's ancestors had clung at the throats of unnumbered moose and caribou and dragged them down, and

68

the wisdom of those ancestors was his. When Leclère's weight came on top of him, he drove his hind legs upward and in, and clawed down chest and abdomen, ripping and tearing through skin and muscle. And when he felt the man's body wince above him and lift, he worried and shook at the man's throat. His teammates closed around in a snarling circle, and Bâtard, with failing breath and fading sense, knew that their jaws were hungry for him. But that did not matter—it was the man, the man above him, and he ripped and clawed, and shook and worried, to the last ounce of his strength. But Leclère choked him with both his hands, till Bâtard's chest heaved and writhed for the air denied, and his eyes glazed and set, and his jaws slowly loosened, and his tongue protruded black and swollen.

'Eh? *Bon*, you devil!' Leclère gurgled, mouth and throat clogged with his own blood, as he shoved the dizzy dog from him.

And then Leclère cursed the other dogs off as they fell upon Bâtard. They drew back into a wider circle, squatting alertly on their haunches and licking their chops, the hair on every neck bristling and erect.

Bâtard recovered quickly, and at the sound of Leclère's voice, tottered to his feet and swayed weakly back and forth.

'A-h-ah! You beeg devil!' Leclère spluttered. 'Ah fix you; Ah fix you plentee, by *Gar*!'

Bâtard, the air biting into his exhausted lungs like wine, flashed full into the man's face, his jaws missing and coming together with a metallic clip. They rolled over and over on the snow, Leclère striking madly with his fists. Then they separated, face to face, and circled back and forth before each other. Leclère could have drawn his knife. His rifle was at his feet. But the beast in him was up and raging. He would do the thing with his hands— and his teeth. Bâtard sprang in, but Leclère knocked him over with a blow of the fist, fell upon him, and buried his teeth to the bone in the dog's shoulder.

It was a primordial setting and a primordial scene, such as might have been in the savage youth of the world. An open space in a dark forest, a ring of grinning wolf-dogs, and in the centre two beasts, locked in combat, snapping and snarling, raging madly about, panting, sobbing, cursing, straining, wild with passion, in a fury of murder, ripping and tearing and clawing in elemental brutishness.

But Leclère caught Bâtard behind the ear, with a blow from his fist, knocking him over, and, for the instant stunning him. Then Leclère leaped upon him with his feet, and sprang up and down, striving to grind him into the earth. Both Bâtard's hind legs were broken ere Leclère ceased that he might catch breath.

'A-a-ah! A-a-ah!' he screamed, incapable of speech, shaking his fist, through sheer impotence of throat and larynx.

But Bâtard was indomitable. He lay there in a helpless welter, his lip feebly lifting and writhing to the snarl he had not the strength to utter. Leclère kicked him, and the tired jaws closed on the ankle, but could not break the skin.

Then Leclère picked up the whip and proceeded almost to cut him to pieces, at each stroke of the last crying: 'Dis taim Ah break you! Eh ? By *Gar !* Ah break you!'

In the end, exhausted, fainting from loss of blood, he crumpled up and fell by his victim, and when the wolf-dogs closed in to take their vengeance, with his last consciousness dragged his body on top of Bâtard to shield him from their fangs.

This occurred not far from Sunrise, and the missionary, opening the door to Leclère a few hours later, was surprised to note the absence of Bâtard from the team. Nor did his surprise lessen when Leclère threw back the robes from the sled, gathered Bâtard into his arms, and staggered across the threshold. It happened that the surgeon of McQuestion, who was something of a gadabout, was up on a gossip, and between them they proceeded to repair Leclère.

'*Merci, non,*' said he. 'Do you fix firs' de dog. To die? *Non.* Eet is not good. Becos' heem Ah mus' yet break. Dat fo' w'at he mus' not die.'

The surgeon called it a marvel, the missionary a miracle, that Leclère pulled through at all; and so weakened was he, that in the spring the fever got him, and he went on his back again. Bâtard had been in even worse plight, but his grip on life prevailed, and the bones of his hind legs knit, and his organs righted themselves, during the several weeks he lay strapped to the floor. And by the time Leclère, finally convalescent, sallow and shaky, took the sun by the cabin door, Bâtard had reasserted his supremacy among his kind, and brought not only his own team-mates but the missionary's dogs into subjection.

He moved never a muscle, nor twitched a hair, when for the first time, Leclère tottered out on the missionary's arm, and sank down slowly and with infinite caution on the three-legged stool.

'*Bon!*' he said. '*Bon!* De good sun.' And he stretched out his wasted hands and washed them in the warmth.

Then his gaze fell on the dog, and the old light blazed back in his eyes. He touched the missionary lightly on the arm. '*Mon père,* dat is one beeg devil, dat Bâtard. You will bring me one pistol, so, dat Ah drink de sun in peace.'

And thenceforth for many days he sat in the sun before the cabin door. He never dozed, and the pistol lay always across his knees. Bâtard had a way, the first thing each day, of looking for the weapon in its wonted place. At sight of it he would lift his lip faintly in token that he understood, and Leclère would lift his own lip in an answering grin. One day the missionary took note of the trick.

'Bless me!' he said. 'I really believe the brute comprehends.'

Leclère laughed softly. 'Look you, *mon père.* Dat w'at Ah now spik, to dat does he lissen.'

71

As if in confirmation, Bâtard just perceptibly wriggled his lone ear up to catch the sound.

'Ah say "keel".'

Bâtard growled deep down in his throat, the hair bristled along his neck, and every muscle went tense and expectant.

'Ah lift de gun, so, like dat.' And suiting action to word, he sighted the pistol at Bâtard.

Bâtard, with a single leap, sideways, landed around the corner of the cabin out of sight.

'Bless me!' he repeated at intervals.

Leclère grinned proudly.

'But why does he not run away?'

The Frenchman's shoulders went up in the racial shrug that means all things from total ignorance to infinite understanding.

'Then why do you not kill him?'

Again the shoulders went up.

'*Mon père*,' he said after a pause, 'de taim is not yet. He is one beeg devil. Some taim Ah break heem, so, an' so, all to leetle bits. Hey? Some taim. *Bon!*'

A day came when Leclère gathered his dogs together and floated down in a bateau to Forty Mile, and on to the Porcupine, where he took a commission from the P.C. Company, and went exploring for the better part of a year. After that he poled up the Koyokuk to deserted Arctic City, and later came drifting back, from camp to camp, along the Yukon. And during the long months Bâtard was well lessoned. He learned many tortures, and, notably, the torture of hunger, the torture of thirst, the torture of fire, and, worst of all, the torture of music.

Like the rest of his kind, he did not enjoy music. It gave him exquisite anguish, racking him nerve by nerve, and ripping apart every fibre of his being. It made him howl, long and wolf-like, as when the wolves bay the stars on frosty nights. He could not help howling. It was his one weakness in the contest with Leclère, and it was his shame. Leclère, on the other hand, passionately loved music—as passionately as he loved strong drink. And when his soul clamoured for expression, it usually uttered itself in one or the other of the two ways, and more usually in both ways. And when he had drunk, his brain a-lilt with unsung song and the devil in him aroused and rampant, his soul found its supreme utterance in torturing Bâtard.

'Now we will haf a leetle museek,' he would say. 'Eh ? W'at you t'ink, Bâtard ?'

It was only an old and battered harmonica, tenderly treasured and patiently repaired; but it was the best that money could buy, and out of its silver reeds he drew weird vagrant airs that men had never heard before. Then Bâtard, dumb of throat, with teeth tight clenched, would back away, inch by inch, to the farthest cabin corner. And Leclère playing, playing, a stout club tucked under his arm, followed the animal up, inch by inch, step by step, till there was no further retreat.

At first Bâtard would crowd himself into the smallest possible space, grovelling close to the floor; but as the music came nearer and nearer, he was forced to uprear, his back jammed into the logs, his fore legs fanning the air as though to beat off the rippling waves of sound. He still kept his teeth together, but severe muscular contractions attacked his body, strange twitchings and jerkings, till he was all a-quiver and writhing in silent torment. As he lost control, his jaws spasmodically wrenched apart, and deep throaty vibrations issued forth, too low in the register of sound for human ear to catch. And then, nostrils distended, eyes dilated, hair bristling in helpless rage, arose the long wolf howl. It came with a slurring rush upward, swelling to a great heart-breaking burst of sound, and dying away in sadly cadenced woe—then the next rush upward, octave upon octave; the bursting heart; and the infinite sorrow and misery, fainting, fading, falling, and dying slowly away.

It was fit for hell. And Leclère, with fiendish ken, seemed to divine each particular nerve and heartstring, and with long wails and tremblings and sobbing minors to make it yield up its last shred of grief. It was frightful, and for twenty-four hours after, Bâtard was nervous and unstrung, starting at common sounds, tripping over his own shadow, but, withal, vicious and masterful with his team-mates. Nor did he show signs of a breaking spirit. Rather did he grow more grim and taciturn, biding his time with an inscrutable patience that began to puzzle and weigh upon Leclère. The dog would lie in the firelight, motionless, for hours, gazing straight before him at Leclère, and hating him with his bitter eyes.

Often the man felt that he had bucked against the very essence of life—the unconquerable essence that swept the hawk down out of the sky like a feathered thunderbolt, that drove the great grey goose across the zones, that hurled the spawning salmon through two thousand miles of boiling Yukon flood. At such times he felt impelled to express his own unconquerable essence; and with strong drink, wild music, and Bâtard, he indulged in vast orgies, wherein he pitted his puny strength in the face of things, and challenged all that was, and had been, and was yet to be.

'Dere is somet'ing dere,' he affirmed, when the rhythmed vagaries of his mind touched the secret chords of Bâtard's being and brought forth the long lugubrious howl. 'Ah pool eet out wid bot' my han's, so, an' so. Ha! Ha! Eet is fonee! Eet is ver' fonee! De priest chant, de womans pray, de mans swear, de leetle bird go *peep-peep*, Bâtard, heem go *yew-yew*—an' eet is all de ver' same t'ing. Ha! Ha!'

Father Gautier, a worthy priest, once reproved him with instances of concrete perdition. He never reproved him again.

'Eet may be so, *mon père*,' he made answer. 'An' Ah t'ink Ah go troo hell a-snappin', lak de hemlock troo de fire. Eh, *mon père?*'

But all bad things come to an end as well as good, and so with

Black Leclère. On the summer low water, in a poling boat, he left McDougall for Sunrise. He left McDougall in company with Timothy Brown, and arrived at Sunrise by himself. Further, it was known that they had quarrelled just previous to pulling out; for the *Lizzie*, a wheezy ten-ton sternwheeler, twenty-four hours behind, beat Leclère in by three days. And when he did get in, it was with a clean-drilled bullet-hole through his shoulder muscle, and a tale of ambush and murder.

A strike had been made at Sunrise, and things had changed considerably. With the infusion of several hundred gold-seekers, a deal of whisky, and half a dozen equipped gamblers, the missionary had seen the page of his years of labour with the Indians wiped clean. When the squaws became preoccupied with cooking beans and keeping the fire going for the wifeless miners, and the bucks with swapping their warm furs for black bottles and broken timepieces, he took to his bed, said 'bless me' several times, and departed to his final accounting in a rough-hewn, oblong box. Whereupon the gamblers moved their roulette and faro tables into the mission house, and the click of chips and clink of glasses went up from dawn till dark and to dawn again.

Now Timothy Brown was well beloved among these adventurers of the North. The one thing against him was his quick temper and ready fist—a little thing, for which his kind heart and forgiving hand more than atoned. On the other hand, there was nothing to atone for Black Leclère. He was 'black', as more than one remembered deed bore witness, while he was as well hated as the other was beloved. So the men of Sunrise put an antiseptic dressing on his shoulder and haled him before Judge Lynch.

It was a simple affair. He had quarrelled with Timothy Brown at McDougall. With Timothy Brown he had left McDougall. Without Timothy Brown he had arrived at Sunrise. Considered in the light of his evilness, the unanimous conclusion was that he had killed Timothy Brown. On the other hand, Leclère

acknowledged their facts, but challenged their conclusion, and gave his own explanation. Twenty miles out of Sunrise he and Timothy Brown were poling the boat along the rocky shore. From that shore two rifle-shots rang out. Timothy Brown pitched out of the boat and went down bubbling red, and that was the last of Timothy Brown. He, Leclère, pitched into the bottom of the boat with a stinging shoulder. He lay very quiet, peeping at the shore. After a time two Indians stuck up their heads and came out to the water's edge, carrying between them a birch-bark canoe. As they launched it, Leclère let fly. He potted one, who went over the side after the manner of Timothy Brown. The other dropped into the bottom of the canoe, and then canoe and poling boat went down the stream in a drifting battle. After that they hung up on a split current, and the canoe passed on one side of an island, the poling boat on the other. That was the last of the canoe, and he came on into Sunrise. Yes, from the way the Indian in the canoe jumped, he was sure he had potted him. That was all.

This explanation was not deemed adequate. They gave him ten hours' grace while the *Lizzie* steamed down to investigate. Ten hours later she came wheezing back to Sunrise. There had been nothing to investigate. No evidence had been found to back up his statements. They told him to make his will, for he possessed a fifty-thousand-dollar Sunrise claim, and they were a law-abiding as well as a law-giving breed.

Leclère shrugged his shoulders. 'Bot one t'ing,' he said; 'a leetle, w'at you call, favour—a leetle favour, dat is eet. I gif my feefty t'ousan' dollair to de church. I gif my husky dog, Bâtard, to de devil. De leetle favour? Fors' you hang heem, an' den you hang me. Eet is good, eh?'

Good it was, they agreed, that Hell's Spawn should break trail for his master across the last divide, and the court was adjourned down to the river-bank, where a big spruce tree stood by itself. Slackwater Charley put a hangman's knot in the end of a hauling-line, and the noose was slipped over Leclère's head and pulled tight around his neck. His hands were tied behind his back, and he was assisted to the top of a cracker box. Then the running end of the line was passed over an overhanging branch, drawn taut, and made fast. To kick the box out from under would leave him dancing on the air.

'Now for the dog,' said Webster Shaw, sometime mining engineer. 'You'll have to rope him, Slackwater.'

Leclère grinned. Slackwater took a chew of tobacco, rove a running noose, and proceeded leisurely to coil a few turns in his hand. He paused once or twice to brush particularly offensive mosquitoes from off his face. Everybody was brushing mosquitoes, except Leclère, about whose head a small cloud was visible. Even Bâtard, lying full-stretched on the ground, with his fore paws rubbed the pests away from eyes and mouth.

But while Slackwater waited for Bâtard to lift his head, a faint call came down the quiet air, and a man was seen waving his arms and running across the flat from Sunrise. It was the storekeeper.

'C-call 'er off, boys,' he panted, as he came in among them.

'Little Sandy and Bernadotte's jes' got in,' he explained with returning breath. 'Landed down below an' come up by the short cut. Got the Beaver with 'im. Picked 'm up in his canoe, stuck in a back channel, with a couple of bullet holes in 'm. Other buck was Klok-Kutz, the one that knocked spots out of his squaw and dusted.'

'Eh ? W'at Ah say ? Eh ?' Leclère cried exultantly. 'Dat de one fo' sure! Ah know Ah spik true.'

'The thing to do is teach these damned Siwashes a little manners,' spoke Webster Shaw. 'They're getting fat and sassy, and we'll have to bring them down a peg. Round in all the bucks and string up the Beaver for an object lesson. That's the programme. Come on and let's see what he's got to say for himself.'

'Heh, *M'sieu'* !' Leclère called, as the crowd began to melt away through the twilight in the direction of Sunrise. 'Ah lak ver' moch to see de fon.'

'Oh, we'll turn you loose when we come back,' Webster Shaw shouted over his shoulder. 'In the meantime meditate on your sins and the ways of providence. It will do you good, so be grateful.'

As is the way with men who are accustomed to great hazards, whose nerves are healthy and trained to patience, so it was with Leclère, who settled himself to the long wait—which is to say that he reconciled his mind to it. There was no settling of the body, for the taut rope forced him to stand rigidly erect. The least relaxation of the leg muscles pressed the rough-fibred noose into his neck, while the upright position caused him much pain in his wounded shoulder. He projected his under lip and expelled his breath upward along his face to blow the mosquitoes away from his eyes. But the situation had its compensation. To be snatched from the maw of death was well worth a little bodily suffering, only it was unfortunate that he should miss the hanging of the Beaver.

And so he mused, till his eyes chanced to fall upon Bâtard, head between fore paws and stretched on the ground asleep. And then Leclère ceased to muse. He studied the animal closely, striving to sense if the sleep were real or feigned. Bâtard's sides were heaving regularly, but Leclère felt that the breath came and went a shade too quickly; also he felt that there was a vigilance or alertness to every hair that belied unshackling sleep. He would have given his Sunrise claim to be assured that the dog was not awake, and once when one of his joints cracked, he looked quickly and guiltily at Bâtard to see if he roused. He did not rouse then, but a few minutes later he got up slowly and lazily, stretched, and looked carefully about him.

'*Sacredam*,' said Leclère, under his breath.

Assured that no one was in sight or hearing, Bâtard sat down, curled his upper lip almost into a smile, looked up at Leclère, and licked his chops.

'Ah see my feenish,' the man said, and laughed sardonically aloud.

Bâtard came nearer, the useless ear wabbling, the good ear cocked forward with devilish comprehension. He thrust his head on one side quizzically, and advanced with mincing, playful steps. He rubbed his body gently against the box till it shook and shook again. Leclère teetered carefully to maintain his equilibrium.

'Bâtard,' he said calmly, 'look out. Ah keel you.'

Bâtard snarled at the word, and shook the box with greater force. Then he upreared, and with is fore paws threw his weight against it higher up. Leclère kicked out with one foot, but the rope bit into his neck and checked so abruptly as nearly to over-balance him.

'Hi, ya! *Chook! Mush-on!*' he screamed.

Bâtard retreated, for twenty feet or so, with a fiendish levity in his bearing that Leclère could not mistake. He remembered the dog often breaking the scum of ice on the water hole, by lifting up and throwing his weight upon it; and, remembering, he understood what he now had in mind. Bâtard faced about and paused. He showed his white teeth in a grin, which Leclère answered; and then hurled his body through the air, in full charge, straight for the box.

Fifteen minutes later, Slackwater Charley and Webster Shaw, returning, caught a glimpse of a ghostly pendulum swinging back and forth in the dim light. As they hurriedly drew in closer, they made out the man's inert body, and a live thing that clung to it, and shook and worried, and gave to it the swaying motion.

'Hi, ya! *Chook!* you Spawn of Hell,' yelled Webster Shaw.

But Bâtard glared at him, and snarled threateningly, without loosing his jaws.

Slackwater Charley got out his revolver, but his hand was shaking, as with a chill, and he fumbled.

'Here, you take it,' he said, passing the weapon over.

Webster Shaw laughed shortly, drew a sight between the gleaming eyes, and pressed the trigger. Bâtard's body twitched with the shock, threshed the ground spasmodically for a moment, and went suddenly limp. But his teeth still held fast locked.

JACK LONDON

Alan Sillitoe

Alan Sillitoe was born in Nottingham, England, in 1928. In the houses of the predominantly working class district where he lived, books were not common but as a boy he managed to build up a small collection of his own, bought mainly from a nearby secondhand shop. These books were important to him because, in his own words: 'Reading was the only means of going into a world other than the one around me, one which I often found disagreeable because it was too close and sometimes too alien'. His interest in books waned, however, when he left school at fourteen to work in the Raleigh Bicycle factory; later he joined the R.A.F. as a wireless operator. At the age of twenty he was forced to spend eighteen months in hospital with tuberculosis. During this period he began to read extensively again and it marked the starting point of his own career as a writer. With the small pension he received when he was invalided from the R.A.F., he decided to travel abroad while he developed his writing.

His first novel, *Saturday Night and Sunday Morning*, won the Authors' Club Award for the best first novel of 1958. It was later made into a film, as was the title story of his second book, a collection of short stories, *The Loneliness of the Long Distance Runner*. Another collection, *The Ragman's Daughter*, was published in 1963. Most of his work is based on his intimate knowledge of working class life in the industrial suburbs. The accuracy with which he captures the atmosphere of the environment, the patterns of speech and the attitudes of this section of society can be seen clearly in 'The Other John Peel' (*Storytellers 1*) and 'The Disgrace of Jim Scarfedale' (*Storytellers 2*). Both of these stories also convey a strong feeling of 'Them and Us'—the difference between working class and middle class.

The Other John Peel

WHEN the world was asleep one Sunday morning Bob slid away from the warm aura of his wife and padded downstairs—boots in hand—to fix up a flask and some bacon sandwiches.

Electric light gave the living-room an ageless air, only different from last night in that it was empty—of people. He looked around at the house full of furniture: television set, washing machine glinting white from the scullery, even a car on the street—the lot, and it belonged to him. Eric and Freda also slept, and he'd promised to take them up the Trent and hire a rowing-boat this afternoon if they were good. Wearing his second-best suit, knapsack all set, he remembered Freda's plea a few days ago: 'Will you bring me one o' them tails, our dad?' He had to laugh, the fawce little bogger, as he combed his dark wavy hair at the mirror and put on his glasses. I must tell her not to blab it to her pals though.

He opened the cellar door for his guns and pouches, put them under his arm to keep them low—having a licence for the twelve-bore, but not the .303 service rifle—and went out into the back-yard. The world was a cemetery on short lease to the night, dead quiet except for the whine of factory generators: a row of upstairs windows were closed tight to hold in the breath of sleep. A pale grey saloon stood by the kerb, the best of several left out on the cobbles, and Bob stowed his guns well down behind the back seat before lighting a cigarette.

83

The streets were yours at six on a Sunday morning, flying through the cradle of a deadbeat world with nothing to stop you getting what fun and excitement you wanted. The one drawback to the .303 was that out of fifty bullets from the army he'd but twenty left, though if he rationed himself to a shot every Sunday there'd still be six months' sport for the taking. And you never knew: maybe he could tap his cousin in the terriers for a belt of souvenirs.

He bounded through the traffic lights, between church and pub, climbing the smooth tarmac up Mansfield Road, then pouring his headlights into the dip and heading north under a sky of stars. Houses fell endlessly back on either side, a gauntlet trying to cup him but getting nowhere. The wireless had forecast a fine day and looked like being right for a change, which was the least they could do for you. It was good to get out after a week cooped-up, to be a long-range hunter in a car that blended with the lanes. He was doing well for himself: wife and kids, a good tool-setting job, and a four-roomed house at fifteen bob a week. Fine. And most Sunday mornings he ranged from Yorkshire to Lincolnshire, and Staffordshire to Leicestershire, every map-point a sitting duck for his coolly sighted guns.

On the dot of six-thirty he saw Ernie by the Valley Road picture house. 'Hey up,' Ernie said as he pulled in. 'That was well timed.' Almost a foot taller than Bob, he loomed over the car dressed in an old mac.

'It's going to be fine,' Bob said, 'according to the radio.'

Ernie let himself in. 'The wireless's allus wrong. Spouts nowt but lies. I got welloes on in case it rains.'

They scooted up the dual carriageway. 'Is this the best you can do?' Ernie asked. 'You can fetch ninety out of this, I'm sure. 'Ark at that engine: purring like a she-cat on the batter.'

'Take your sweat,' Bob said. 'This is a mystery trip.'

Ernie agreed. 'I'm glad there's no racing on a Sunday. It's good to get out a bit like this.'

'It is, an' all. Missis well?'

'Not too bad. Says she feels like a battleship with such a big belly'—and went silent. Bob knew him well enough: he'd never talk just to be friendly; they could drive for an hour and he'd stay shut, often in an icy far-off mood that didn't give him anything to say or think of. They worked a dozen feet from each other all week, Bob on his precision jobs, Ernie watching a row of crank-shift millers. 'What guns you got then?' he asked.

Bob peered ahead, a calm and measured glance along the lit-up wastes of the road to Ollerton. 'A twelve-bore and a .303.'

'I wish you had,' Ernie laughed. 'You never know when you're going to need a .303 these days. Best gun out.'

'Keep your trap shut about it though,' Bob said. 'I got it in the army. I wouldn't tell you except that I know I can trust you by now.'

Maybe he wasn't joking, Ernie thought. Bob was clever with hands and brain, the stop-gap of the shop with micrometer and centre-lathe, a toolmaker who could turn off a candlestick or fag-lighter as soon as look at you. 'Do you mean it about a .303 ?'

Bob pulled into a lay-by and got out. 'Keep clear of the head-lights,' he said, 'but catch this.' Ernie caught it, pushed forward the safety catch, the magazine resting in the net of his fingers. 'God Almighty! Anything up the spout ?'

'I've a clip in my pocket. Strictly for rabbits'—Bob smiled, taking it back.

'A waste,' Ernie said. 'The twelve-bore would do. Mixer-matosis has killed 'em all off, anyway.'

They drove on. 'Had it since I left the army,' Bob told him. 'The stores was in a chronic state in Germany at the end of the war. Found myself with two, so kept one. I have a pot-shot with it now and again. I enjoy hunting—for a bit o' recreation.'

Ernie laughed, wildly and uncontrolled, jerking excited shouts into the air as if trying to throw something out of his mouth, hold-ing his stomach to stop himself doubling up, wearing down the shock of what a free-lance .303 meant. He put his arm around Bob's shoulder by way of congratulation: 'You'd better not let many people know about it, or the coppers'll get on to you.'

'Don't worry. If ever they search, it's a souvenir. I'd get rid of the bolt, and turn another off on the lathe when I needed it.'

'Marvellous,' Ernie said. 'A .303! Just the thing to have in case of a revolution. I hope I can get my hands on one when the trouble starts.'

Bob was sardonic: 'You and your revolution! There wain't be one in our lifetimes, I can tell you that.' Ernie had talked revolu-tion to him for months, had argued with fiery puritanical force, guiding Bob's opinion from voting Labour to a head-nodding acceptance of rough and ready Communism. 'I can't see why you think there'll be a revolution though.'

'I've told you though,' Ernie said loudly. 'There's got to be something. I feel it. We wok in a factory, don't we? Well, we're the backbone of the country, but you see, Bob, there's too many people on our backs. And it's about time they was slung off. The last strike we had a bloke in a pub said to me: 'Why are you fellows allus on strike?' And I said to 'im: 'What sort o' work do you do?' And he said: 'I'm a travelling salesman.' So I said, ready to smash 'im: 'Well, the reason I come out on strike is because I want to get bastards like yo' off my back.' That shut 'im up. He just crawled back into his sherry.'

At dawn they stopped the car in a ladle of land between Tuxford and the Dukeries, pulling on to a grass verge by a gate. A tall hawthorn hedge covered in green shoots bordered the lane, and the bosom of the meadow within rose steeply to a dark skyline, heavy rolls of cloud across it. Ernie stood by the gate: 'The clouds smell fresh'—pulling his mac collar up. 'Think we'll get owt 'ere?'

'It's good hunting country' Bob told him. 'I know for a fact.'

They opened flasks and tore hungrily into sandwiches. 'Here, have a swig of this,' Ernie said, pouring some into his own cup. 'It'll do you good.'

Bob held it to the light. 'What is it?'

'Turps and dash. Here's the skin off your lips.'

'Don't talk so loud. You'll chase all the wild life away. Not a bad drop, is it?'

'A rabbit wouldn't get far with a .303 cracking away behind it.' A sort of loving excitement paralysed his fingers when he picked up the rifle: 'Can you get me one?'

'They don't grow on trees, Ernie.'

'I'd like one, though. For the next war. I'd just wait for somebody to try and call me up!' They leaned on the gate, smoking. 'Christ, when the Russians come I'll be liberated.'

'It's a good job everybody ain't like you,' Bob said with a smile. 'You're a rare 'un, yo' are.'

Ernie saw a movement across the field, beginning from the right and parting a diagonal line of grass, ascending towards the crest on their left. The light from behind showed it up clear and neat. 'See it?' he hissed, ramming a shell in the twelve-bore. Bob said nothing, noiselessly lifted the .303. No need to use that, Ernie thought. It'd bring a man down a mile off: a twelve-bore's good enough for a skinful of mixer-matosis.

A sudden wind blew against the dawn, ruffling the line of their prey. Bob's eye was still on it: a single round went into the breech. 'I'll take it,' he said softly. It was already out of buck-shot from Ernie's twelve-bore. Both lost it, but said nothing. A lull in the wind didn't show it up. 'I expect it's a hare.'

Bob lowered his .303, but Ernie signalled him to be quiet: it seemed as if a match were lit in the middle of the field, a slow-burning brown flame moving cautiously through shallow grass, more erratic now, but still edging towards the crest. The cold, star-flecked sky needed only a slow half turn to bring full day-light. What the bloody hell is it? Ernie wondered. Fields and lane were dead quiet: they were kings of the countryside: no houses, no one in sight. He strained his eyes hoping to discover what it was. A squirrel? Some gingernut, anyway.

A smile came on to Bob's face, as when occasionally at work his patience paid off over some exacting job, a flange going into place with not half a thou' to spare. Now it was more heightened than that: a triumph of hunting. Two sharp ears were seen on the sky-line, a hang-dog tail, a vulpine mouth breakfasting on wind— with Ernie's heart a bongo drum playing rhythms on his chest wall: a fox.

The air split open, and from all directions came a tidal wave of noise, rushing in on every ear but that to which the bullet had been aimed. Together they were over the gate, and speeding up

the slope as if in a dawn attack. Gasping, Bob knelt and turned the dead fox over: as precise a job as he had ever done. 'I always get 'em in the head if I can. I promised one of the tails to a neighbour'.

'Ain't this the first fox you've shot, then?' Ernie couldn't fathom his quiet talk: a fox stone-dead from a .303 happened once in a lifetime. They walked down the hill. 'I've had about half a dozen,' he said by the car door, dragging a large polythene bag from under the seat and stuffing the dead fox into it. 'From round here most on 'em. I'll knock off a bit and go to Lincolnshire next time.' The fox lay as if under a glass case, head bashed and tail without colour. 'It never stood a chance with a .303,' Ernie grinned.

He took the wheel going back, flying down lanes to the main road, setting its nose at Mansfield as if intent on cutting Nottinghamshire in two. Bob lounged behind using a pull-through on the .303. 'I've allus liked hunting,' he shouted to Ernie. 'My old man used to go poaching before the war, so we could have summat to eat. He once did a month in quod, the poor bastard. Never got a chance to enjoy real hunting, like me.'

'I want the next tail, for the kid that's coming,' Ernie said, laughing.

Bob was pleased with himself: 'You talk about revolution: the nobs around here would go daft if they knew I was knocking their sport off.'

It was broad daylight: 'Have another turps and dash,' Ernie said, 'you clever bleeder. You'll find the bottle in my haversack.'

The road opened along a high flat ridge through a colliery, whose grey houses still had no smoke at their chimneys. Silent headstocks to the left towered above the fenced-off coppices of Sherwood Forest.

ALAN SILLITOE

O. Henry

O. Henry (William Sydney Porter) was born in America in 1867. His first job was on a ranch in Texas. He then joined the staff of a newspaper and only a year later bought his own newspaper business. This proved to be a failure, however, and shortly afterwards he went to Central America. On his return to Texas, he worked for a while in a drug store; he then moved to New Orleans, where for the first time he began to concentrate on his writing. Finally he moved to New York, where he remained until his death in 1910. He died 'of a slow and wasting disease' just as he was achieving real success and recognition as a writer. Although he never wrote a novel—the nearest to one was the volume *Cabbages and Kings*—he produced over a dozen books containing some 270 stories, most of which can now be found in omnibus editions of his work.

His supreme ability to provide, often in the very last sentence of a story, a totally unexpected conclusion had a considerable influence on the development of the short story. But, unlike less talented exponents of the surprise ending, he never allowed the complications of the plot to overrule other important qualities such as convincing characterisation and atmosphere. Many modern writers shun the trick plot on the grounds that it is untrue to life. Nevertheless, it is a technique requiring considerable skill: characters and situations must be real enough for us to accept, but not so authentic that the twist at the end seems artificial. 'Jeff Peters as a Personal Magnet' (*Storytellers 1*) and 'Science of Matrimony' (*Storytellers 2*) both demonstrate how complete was O. Henry's mastery of this technique.

Jeff Peters as a Personal Magnet

JEFF PETERS has been engaged in as many schemes for making money as there are recipes for cooking rice in Charleston, S.C.

Best of all I like to hear him tell of his earlier days when he sold liniments and cough cures on street corners, living hand to mouth, heart to heart, with the people, throwing heads or tails with fortune for his last coin.

'I struck Fisher Hill, Arkansaw,' said he, 'in a buckskin suit, mocoasins, long hair and a thirty-carat diamond ring that I got from an actor in Texarkana. I don't know what he ever did with the pocket-knife I swapped him for it.

'I was Dr. Waugh-hoo, the celebrated Indian medicine man. I carried only one best bet just then, and that was Resurrection Bitters. It was made of life-giving plants and herbs accidentally discovered by Ta-qua-la, the beautiful wife of the chief of the Choctaw Nation, while gathering truck to garnish a platter of boiled dog for the annual corn dance.

'Business hadn't been good at the last town, so I only had five dollars. I went to the Fisher Hill druggist and he credited me for half a gross of eight-ounce bottles and corks. I had the labels and ingredients in my valise, left over from the last town. Life began to look rosy again after I got in my hotel room with the water running from the tap, and the Resurrection Bitters lining up on the table by the dozen.

'Fake? No sir. There was two dollars' worth of fluid extract of cinchoma and a dime's worth of aniline in that half-gross of bitters. I've gone through towns years afterwards and had folks ask for 'em again.

'I hired a wagon that night and commenced selling the bitters on Main Street. Fisher Hill was a low, malarial town; and a compound hypothetical pneumocardiac anti-scorbutic tonic was just what I diagnosed the crowd as needing. The bitters started off like sweetbreads-on-toast at a vegetarian dinner. I had sold two dozen at fifty cents apiece when I felt somebody pull my coat tail. I knew what that meant; so I climbed down and sneaked a five-dollar bill into the hand of a man with a German silver star on his lapel.

' "Constable," says I, "it's a fine night."

' "Have you got a city licence," he asks, "to sell this illegitimate essence of spooju that you flatter by the name of medicine ?"

' "I have not," says I. "I didn't know you had a city. If I can find it tomorrow I'll take one out if it's necessary."

' "I'll have to close you up till you do," says the constable.

'I quit selling and went back to the hotel. I was talking to the landlord about it.

' "Oh, you won't stand no show in Fisher Hill," says he. "Dr. Hoskins, the only doctor here, is a brother-in-law of the Mayor, and they don't allow no fake doctor to practise in town."

' "I don't practise medicine," says I, "I've got a State pedlar's licence, and I take out a city one wherever they demand it."

'I went to the Mayor's office the next morning and they told me he hadn't showed up yet. They didn't know when he'd be down. So Doc Waugh-hoo hunches down again in a hotel chair and lights a jimpson-weed regalia, and waits.

'By and by a young man in a blue neck-tie slips into the chair next to me and asks the time.

' "Half-past ten," says I, "and you are Andy Tucker. I've seen you work. Wasn't it you that put up the Great Cupid Combination

94

package on the Southern States? Let's see, it was a Chilian diamond engagement ring, a wedding-ring, a potato masher, a bottle of soothing syrup and Dorothy Vernon—all for fifty cents."

'Andy was pleased to hear that I remembered him. He was a good street man; and he was more than that—he respected his profession, and he was satisfied with 300 per cent profit. He had plenty of offers to go into the illegitimate drug and garden seed business; but he was never to be tempted off of the straight path.

'I wanted a partner; so Andy and me agreed to go out together. I told him about the situation in Fisher Hill and how finances was low on account of the local mixture of politics and jalap. Andy had just got in on the train that morning. He was pretty low himself, and was going to canvass the town for a few dollars to build a new battleship by popular subscription at Eureka Springs. So we went out and sat on the porch, and talked it over.

'The next morning at eleven o'clock, when I was sitting there alone, an Uncle Tom shuffles into the hotel and asked for the doctor to come and see Judge Banks, who, it seems, was the mayor and a mighty sick man.

' "I'm no doctor," says I. "Why don't you go and get the doctor?"

' "Boss," says he, "Doc Hoskins am done gone twenty miles in de country to see some sick persons. He's de only doctor in de town, and Massa Banks am powerful bad off. He sent me to ax you to please, suh, come."

' "As man to man," says I, "I'll go and look him over." So I put a bottle of Resurrection Bitters in my pocket and goes up on the hill to the Mayor's mansion, the finest house in town, with a mansard roof and two cast-iron dogs on the lawn.

'This Mayor Banks was in bed all but his whiskers and feet. He was making internal noises that would have had everybody in San Francisco hiking for the parks. A young man was standing by the bed holding a cup of water.

' "Doc," says the Mayor, "I'm awful sick. I'm about to die. Can't you do nothing for me ?"

' "Mr. Mayor," says I, "I'm not a regular pre-ordained disciple of S. Q. Lapius. I never took a course in a medical college," says I, "I've just come as a fellow-man to see if I could be of assistance."

' "I'm deeply obliged," says he. "Doc Waugh-hoo, this is my nephew, Mr. Biddle. He has tried to alleviate my distress, but without success. Oh, Lordy! Ow-ow-ow!!" he sings out.

'I nods at Mr. Biddle and sets down by the bed and feels the Mayor's pulse. "Let me see your liver—your tongue, I mean," says I. Then I turns up the lids of his eyes and looks close at the pupils of 'em.

' "How long have you been sick ?" I asked.

' "I was taken down—ow-ouch—last night," says the Mayor. "Gimme something for it, doc, won't you ?"

' "Mr. Fiddle," says I, "raise the window shade a bit, will you ?"

' "Biddle," says the young man. "Do you feel like you could eat some ham and eggs, Uncle James ?"

' "Mr. Mayor," says I, after laying my ear to his right shoulder-blade and listening, "you've got a bad attack of super-inflammation of the right clavicle of the harpsichord!"

' "Good Lord!" says he, with a groan. "Can't you rub something on it, or set it or anything ?"

'I picks up my hat and starts for the door.

' "You ain't going, doc ?" says the Mayor with a howl. "You ain't going away and leave me to die with this—superfluity of the clapboards, are you ?"

' "Common humanity, Dr. Whoa-ha," says Mr. Biddle, "ought to prevent your deserting a fellow-human in distress."

' "Dr. Waugh-hoo, when you get through ploughing," says I. And then I walks back to the bed and throws back my long hair.

' "Mr. Mayor," says I, "there is only one hope for you. Drugs will do you no good. But there is another power higher yet, although drugs are high enough," says I.

' "And what is that ?" says he.

' "Scientific demonstrations," says I. "The triumph of mind over sarsaparilla. The belief that there is no pain and sickness except what is produced when we ain't feeling well. Declare yourself in arrears. Demonstrate."

' "What is this paraphernalia you speak of, doc ?" says the Mayor. "You ain't a Socialist, are you ?"

' "I am speaking," says I, "of the great doctrine of psychic financiering—of the enlightened school of long-distance, subconscientious treatment of fallacies and meningitis—of that wonderful indoor sport known as personal magnetism."

' "Can you work it, doc ?" asks the Mayor.

' "I'm one of the Sole Sanhedrims and Ostensible Hooplas of the Inner Pulpit," says I. "The lame talk and the blind rubber whenever I make a pass at 'em. I am a medium, a coloratura hypnotist and a spirituous control. It was only through me at the recent séances at Ann Arbour that the late president of the Vinegar Bitters Company could revisit the earth to communicate with his sister Jane. You see me peddling medicine on the streets," says I, "to the poor. I don't practise personal magnetism on them. I do not drag it in the dust," says I, "because they haven't got the dust."

' "Will you treat my case ?" asks the Mayor.

' "Listen," says I. "I've had a good deal of trouble with medical societies everywhere I've been. I don't practise medicine. But, to save your life, I'll give you the psychic treatment if you'll agree as mayor not to push the licence question."

' "Of course I will," says he. "And now get to work, doc, for them pains are coming on again."

' "My fee will be $250.00, cure guaranteed in two treatments," says I.

' "All right," says the Mayor. "I'll pay it. I guess my life's worth that much."

'I sat down by the bed and looked him straight in the eye.

' "Now," says I, "get your mind off the disease. You ain't sick. You haven't got a heart or a clavicle or a funny-bone or brains or anything. You haven't got any pain. Declare error. Now you feel the pain that you didn't have leaving, don't you?"

' "I do feel some little better, doc," says the Mayor, "darned if I don't. Now state a few lies about my not having this swelling in my left side, and I think I could be propped up and have some sausage and buckwheat cakes."

'I made a few passes with my hands.

' "Now," says I, "the inflammation's gone. The right lobe of the perihelion has subsided. You're getting sleepy. You can't hold your eyes open any longer. For the present the disease is checked. Now, you are asleep."

'The Mayor shut his eyes slowly and began to snore.

' "You observe, Mr. Tiddle," says I, "the wonders of modern science."

' "Biddle," says he. "When will you give uncle the rest of the treatment, Dr. Pooh-pooh?"

' "Waugh-hoo," says I. 'I'll come back at eleven tomorrow. When he wakes up give him eight drops of turpentine and three pounds of steak. Good morning."

'The next morning I went back on time. "Well, Mr. Riddle," says I, when he opened the bedroom door, "and how is uncle this morning?"

' "He seems much better," says the young man.

'The Mayor's colour and pulse was fine. I gave him another treatment, and he said the last of the pain left him.

' "Now," says I, "you'd better stay in bed for a day or two, and you'll be all right. It's a good thing I happened to be in Fisher Hill, Mr. Mayor," says I, "for all the remedies in the cornucopia that the regular schools of medicine use couldn't have saved you. And now that error has flew and pain proved a perjurer, let's allude to a cheerfuller subject—say the fee of $250. No cheques, please; I hate to write my name on the back of a cheque almost as bad as I do on the front."

' "I've got the cash here," says the Mayor, pulling a pocket-book from under his pillow.

'He counts out five fifty-dollar notes and holds 'em in his hand.

' "Bring the receipt," he says to Biddle.

'I signed the receipt and the Mayor handed me the money. I put it in my inside pocket careful.

' "Now do your duty, officer," says the Mayor, grinning much unlike a sick man.

'Mr. Biddle lays his hand on my arm.

' "You're under arrest, Dr. Waugh-hoo, alias Peters," says he, "for practising medicine without authority under the State law."

' "Who are you?" I asks.

' "I'll tell you who he is," says Mr. Mayor, sitting up in bed. "He's a detective employed by the State Medical Society. He's been following you over five counties. He came to me yesterday and we fixed up this scheme to catch you. I guess you won't do any more doctoring around these parts, Mr. Faker. What was it you said I had, doc?" the Mayor laughs, "compound—well it wasn't softening of the brain, I guess, anyway."

' "A detective," says I.

' "Correct," says Biddle. "I'll have to turn you over to the sheriff."

' "Let's see you do it," says I, and I grabs Biddle by the throat and half throws him out of the window, but he pulls a gun and sticks it under my chin, and I stand still. Then he puts handcuffs on me, and takes the money out of my pocket.

' "I witness," says he, "that they're the same bills that you and I marked, Judge Banks. I'll turn them over to the sheriff when we get to his office, and he'll send you a receipt. They'll have to be used as evidence in the case."

' "All right, Mr. Biddle," says the Mayor. "And now, Doc Waugh-hoo," he goes on, "why don't you demonstrate? Can't you pull the cork out of your magnetism with your teeth and hocus-pocus them handcuffs off?"

' "Come on, officer," says I, dignified. "I may as well make the best of it." And then I turns to old Banks and rattles my chains.

' "Mr. Mayor," says I, "the time will come soon when you'll believe that personal magnetism is a success. And you'll be sure that it succeeded in this case, too."

'And I guess it did.

'When we got nearly to the gate, I says: "We might meet somebody now, Andy. I reckon you better take 'em off, and——" Hey? Way, of course it was Andy Tucker. That was his scheme; and that's how we got the capital to go into business together.'

O. HENRY

Angus Wilson

Angus Wilson was born in 1913, and spent his childhood in South Africa. A public school education in England was followed by three years at Oxford University. He then joined the staff of the British Museum. During the war he worked in the Foreign Office; afterwards he returned to the British Museum, where he had the important job of replacing the thousands of books lost in the bombing. He did not begin writing until he was thirty-three; his first two books, *The Wrong Set* and *Such Darling Dodos*, both collections of short stories, were published in 1949 and 1950 respectively. His first novel, *Hemlock and After*, appeared in 1953 and a third book of short stories, *A Bit Off the Map*, in 1957. He left the British Museum in 1955 to devote more time to writing; since 1963, however, he has combined this with teaching at the University of East Anglia. In addition to novels and short stories, he has written a number of plays and non-fictional works.

The settings and characters in his stories reflect to a large extent his own middle class background. 'Higher Standards' (*Storytellers 1*) is fairly typical of the subtle way in which he describes and analyses relationships, ruthlessly exposing human weaknesses but still retaining a degree of compassion for his subjects. 'Mummy to the Rescue' (*Storytellers 2*) also shows the same qualities but the conclusion is something of a departure from the normal structure of his stories.

Higher Standards

'COME along then, both,' said Mrs. Corfe. It had been the form of her call to tea at half-past six every evening for more than fifteen years. Perhaps it had lost some of its accuracy since Mr. Corfe's stroke some four years before, but home would not have been the same without it; and, if Mrs. Corfe's conception of 'home' was a trifle ill-defined, her determination that it should never be other than 'the same' was the central thread of all her actions and words.

There was nothing to upset her mother's love of sameness in her daughter's slow response to her call. It merely meant that Elsie had come home in one of her moods. There was a time, of course, before the war when Elsie had not had 'moods'. Indeed, there was a sort of tacit agreement between mother and daughter that the blackness of these moods should be indicated by the length of time that Elsie remained in her bedroom after the summons to meals. If, as on that evening, Mrs. Corfe had time to hoist her husband from his chair and support him doll-like on his dangling legs to the loaded table, before her daughter appeared at the foot of the stairs peering myopically with refined distaste at the jelly and the jam puffs, then it was clearly one of Elsie's bad evenings. Not that this particularly distressed Mrs. Corfe, for it allowed her to say brightly, 'Waiting for late folk never made an egg fresher or the tea hotter.'

Elsie's rejoinder to the implied moral rebuke was aesthetic. She carefully removed one by one from the overcrowded table the many half empty pots of jam and bottles of sauce without which her mother felt the evening meal to be incomplete. Then, going to the mirror, she set the little lemon *crepe de Chine* scarf she wore in the evenings into pretty artistic folds; she further asserted her more refined canons of taste by loosening the beech leaves in the vase on the mantlepiece. Such autumn decoration was the sole incursion on the more traditional furnishing of the parlour that her rebellion had ever achieved. Her mother's revenge came each morning when she crammed the branches back into the vase.

Boiled eggs in egg-cups shaped like kittens and roosters were followed by a 'grunter', a traditional local dish to which, under the stress of rationing, Mrs. Corfe had become increasingly attached. Originally designed as a baked suet roll to contain strips of pork or bacon, it had become a convenient receptacle for all unattractive scraps. Mrs. Corfe, however, retained the humour of the tradition by inserting two burnt currants for the pig's eyes and a sprig of parsley for its tail.

Elsie, like her mother in so many things, shared her love of quaint local customs; but the 'grunter' was a whimsy against which her stomach had long revolted at the end of a tiring day's teaching. She selected three brussel-sprouts and, cutting them very exactly into four parts each, chewed them very carefully with her front teeth. Mrs. Corfe ate heartily, continually spearing fresh pieces of the 'grunter' with her knife. The noise of her mother's feeding brought to Elsie's pale features a fixed expression of attention to higher things.

Neither her daughter's aura of self-pity nor her own pre-occupation with feeding in any way inhibited Mrs. Corfe's continuous flow of talk. After a day of housework and sick nursing, she looked forward to her daughter's return with a greed that was almost physical. To scatter the weariness and frustration of life's daily round in an evening's censorious gossip, to indulge herself in little disapproving jokes about less thrifty, less respectable

neighbours seemed the least that so many years of godly living and duty and deadening physical labour might be expected to give to a tired old woman. It was perhaps her only real grudge against Elsie that the girl refused to apply to her jaded nerves the sharp restorative of a little vinegary talk about her neighbours. How soon these black moods would pass from her daughter, she reflected, if only she would allow herself the soothing easement of village scandal or discharge the heavy burdened soul in a righteous jibe or two.

'Carters have refused to serve "The Laurels" again,' she said. 'The woman's half distracted. It's nice enough to have grand folk from London coming for the weekend; it's another thing to feed them from an empty larder. Oh!' she drew in her breath with disapproving relish. 'The woman's been on the telephone all day to the other shops. She'll make use of *that* at any rate until it's cut off. But for any effect it's had, she might have saved her breath. On *one* tradesman's black books, on *all*. There might be a pint of milk and a plate of porridge for the city folks *if* they're lucky,' she paused for a second and then added, 'and there might not. But still she's got her fur coat to keep her warm outside, if there's no soup to cheer the inner man.'

Elsie tried hard not to envy Mrs. Hardy her musquash. She pictured as vividly as she could the vulgarity, the terrible, clashing bright colours of the drawing-room at "The Laurels" when she attended the Red Cross committee meetings there. But it was no good, she wanted the fur coat.

Mrs. Corfe tried another tack. If the punishment of the godless brought no comfort, then the distresses of the back-sliding would surely answer.

'It's been a day of wonders at the Fitchett's,' she announced with mock solemnity. 'At eight o'clock our Bess had won ten thousand on the Pools. It was *pounds* then, but when the morning post brought nothing, it was down to shillings. All the same the old man quite bit Miss Rennett's head off when she mentioned principles. Nothing against Pools in The Book, it seems. But when the afternoon post went by, there was quite a change around. Nasty, ungodly things the Pools. Mrs. Fitchett's given our Bess a talking to, so we'll have *her* yellow bonnet back in Chapel next Sunday. Ah! well, it takes more than the Fitchetts and such turnabouts to change the ways of old Nick.'

Elsie remembered the lecture she had given to Standard Four only that morning against gambling. Television and Pools and Space Robots, that was all the children of today thought about. But somewhere at the back of her vision a tall, dark stranger leaned over to loosen her sable wrap for her as she settled herself in the gondola.

'How heavenly St. Mark's looks tonight,' she said with exquisite taste, and, '*Our* St. Mark's,' he replied.

Of course, the Pools were a terrible drain on the nation's decency, but . . .

Mrs. Corfe was playing her last card now in the macabre vein. She had almost finished the jelly, and soon it would be time to put Father to bed, so there was not a moment to lose if the evening was to bring any cosy exchange.

'They doubt,' she said, 'if old Mary will last the night. The poor old soul's been wandering terribly, and bringing up every scrap she's taken...'

But Elsie had endured enough of the sordid aspects of life. She leaned across the table, speaking very distinctly:

'And what did *you* do today, Father?' she asked.

A twitch of anger shot through Mrs. Corfe's wrinkled cheek. Now that *was* selfish of Elsie, selfish and thoughtless. Her father who had been such a fine man, so hard-working and thrifty, and such a splendid lay preacher, too, for all that he'd had no education. What had he *done* today, indeed? What *could* he do since this wicked thing had struck him? And what indeed could *she* do but keep him neat and clean before their neighbours as he would have wished.

'Well, gel,' Mr. Corfe replied, 'I sat up at back window and watched the fowls. It's a wonder the way that crookity-backed one gets the scraps. Why should *she* have had the crooked back, I asked myself. Oh, the ways of Providence are strange: all they fowls and only one crookity backed, and yet she gets her share. There's a thing to think upon, and to talk upon...'

'Yes, yes, indeed,' said Mrs. Corfe, 'but not now'. It shamed her that her husband who had always been so clear in his thoughts, so upstanding, should at last wander so unsuitably in his words. Elsie, too, felt the need to protect her father from what his failing body had made him; and so, when her mother began to question her on the events at school that day, she forced herself to answer.

'It's been a Standard IV day for you I know, my girl, by your tired looks,' said Mrs. Corfe. And when Elsie began to recount the exploits of that famous undisciplined class, her mother listened avidly. Such sad happenings, such examples of human frailty in the nearby town, were second only to village misdemeanours in her catalogue of pleasures.

'Ah! the Mardykes, I thought they'd be somewhere in it. There's a couple of old Nick's own that'll come to sorry ends,' she said with fervour, when Elsie mentioned the notorious bad boys of the form. 'And the woman had sent them out with nothing but a rumble in their stomachs for breakfast, I'll be bound.' It was the fecklessness of city workers that so fascinated Mrs. Corfe. And then, as though her bitterness had sated itself, she added, 'You must take them some apples tomorrow, Elsie. They're a couple of comics if ever there were any.'

'Miss Teasdale's away with the flu,' said Elsie, 'so I've got *her* handful to deal with, too.'

'And why can't they get a Supply in?' asked her mother impatiently.

'Supply teachers need notification. Why do you use words you don't understand?' Elsie asked angrily.

It was lucky that noises in the village street came so suddenly to prevent a family quarrel. Shrill whistles could be heard, loud shouting, the sharp swerve of bicycle wheels followed by guffaws of coarse laughter.

'H'm,' said Mrs. Corfe. 'Well, there's *our* Standard IV anyway.' It was their favourite name for the youths who nightly rode the length of the village street to call after girls.

Half an hour later when Elsie went to the pillar-box with a letter to an old friend of her Teacher's Training College days, a group of these young men were leaning on the nearby fence. Well! she thought, Bill Daly and Jim Soker among them, they ought to be ashamed wasting their time like that. At their age, too. Why, Jim was a year older than herself, quite twenty-six. She was about to pass by with her usual self-conscious, majestic disregard, when her loneliness was shot through with an aching for those childhood days before awakening prudery and her scholarship to the 'County' had cut her off from the village Standard IV. She paused for a moment at the pillar-box and looked back at them. One of the younger boys let out a wolf whistle, but Bill Daly stopped him short.

'Hallo, Elsie,' he said in the usual imitation American, 'how about a little walk?'

The retort came easily to Elsie's lips, 'Does teacher know you're out of school, Bill Daly?' she said; but the words came strangely—not in her customary school-marm tone, but with a long-buried, common, cheeky giggle. She even smiled and waved, and her walk as she left them was almost tarty in its jauntiness. She was tempted to look back, but another wolf whistle recalled her to her superior taste, her isolated social position in the village.

Mrs. Corfe had her old black outdoor coat on, when Elsie returned.

'Who was that you were talking to?' she asked.

'Oh! Standard IV,' Elsie answered, 'Bill Daly was there. He ought to be ashamed fooling about like that at his age.'

'Well, it's lucky there are folks with *higher* standards,' said her mother. 'Father's not too good,' she added, 'the "grunter's" turned on him. I'm just off down to old Mary's. I've promised to sit with the poor creature. It may help to keep the bogies away.'

Elsie's outing seemed to have softened her mood. She touched her mother's arm. 'You do too much for them all,' she said.

'Oh! well,' Mrs. Corfe replied gruffly, 'if the poor won't help the poor, I'd like to know who will. I don't like leaving your father though...'

Through the flat acceptance of their life implied in her mother's tone came once more the wolf whistles and guffaws, and mingled with them now the high giggle of the village girls. Elsie's laugh was hard and hysterical. 'Oh! don't fuss, so, mother,' she cried, 'I'll sit up with father. You haven't got a monopoly of higher standards, you know.'

ANGUS WILSON

Ray Bradbury

Ray Bradbury was born in the U.S.A., in Waukegan, Illinois, in 1920. He was educated in Los Angeles, where he still lives. He has been writing science fiction since he was twelve and has evolved a unique, richly coloured style, full of haunting, poetic images. When once asked about his writing methods, he replied: 'I write because I love writing. I'm not a thinker . . . My logic is all in my emotions.' This is not to say that his work is lacking in abstract ideas. Many of his stories, particularly those set in the future, show a profound concern with the challenge presented to humanity by our ever-expanding technology. (Will these inventions improve our lives or rule them?). 'The Murderer' (*Storytellers 2*), for example, although light-hearted in tone, still makes a serious observation on a possible development of our society and the place of the individual within it. 'A Sound of Thunder' (*Storytellers 1*) can be enjoyed simply as a good adventure yarn but it also demonstrates how delicate is the balance of our environment.

Both the above stories come from the collection *The Golden Apples of the Sun*, which contains a wide selection of Bradbury's work: there are science fiction stories with underlying social comment, tales of fantasy, and 'straight' stories set in the present. The contents of *The October Country* may be loosely described as dealing with 'horror and imagination', and their eerie mood is well illustrated by Joe Mugnani. *Farenheit 451* is set in a world where books are forbidden and where private thought and action are criminal; the rebellion of the hero, Montag, provides an exciting and thought-provoking story, which warns us, as do many of Bradbury's stories, of the dangers of submitting to the continual assaults that are made on the world of our imagination. His other books include *The Illustrated Man* (which has been made into a film), *The Day it Rained Forever*, and *The Silver Locusts*.

A Sound of Thunder

THE sign on the wall seemed to quaver under a film of sliding warm water. Eckels felt his eyelids blink over his stare, and the sign burned in this momentary darkness:

> TIME SAFARI, INC.
>
> SAFARIS TO ANY YEAR IN THE PAST.
>
> YOU NAME THE ANIMAL.
>
> WE TAKE YOU THERE.
>
> YOU SHOOT IT.

A warm phlegm gathered in Eckel's throat; he swallowed and pushed it down. The muscles around his mouth formed a smile as he put his hand slowly out upon the air, and in that hand waved a cheque for ten thousand dollars to the man behind the desk.

'Does this safari guarantee I come back alive ?'

'We guarantee nothing,' said the official, 'except the dinosaurs.' He turned. 'This is Mr. Travis, your Safari Guide in the Past. He'll tell you what and where to shoot. If he says no shooting, no shooting. If you disobey instructions, there's a stiff penalty of another ten thousand dollars, plus possible government action, on your return.'

Eckels glanced across the vast office at a mass and tangle, a snaking and humming of wires and steel boxes, at an aurora that flickered now orange, now silver, now blue. There was a sound like a gigantic bonfire burning all of Time, all the years and all the parchment calendars, all the hours piled high and set aflame.

A touch of the hand and this burning would, on the instant, beautifully reverse itself. Eckels remembered the wording in the advertisements to the letter. Out of chars and ashes, out of dust and coals, like golden salamanders, the old years, the green years, might leap; roses sweeten the air, white hair turn Irish-black, wrinkles vanish; all, everything fly back to seed, flee death, rush down to their beginnings, suns rise in western skies and set in glorious easts, moons eat themselves opposite to the custom, all and everything cupping one in another like Chinese boxes, rabbits into hats, all and everything returning to the fresh death, the seed death, the green death, to the time before the beginning. A touch of a hand might do it, the merest touch of a hand.

'Hell and damn,' Eckels breathed, the light of the Machine on his thin face. 'A real Time Machine.' He shook his head. 'Makes you think. If the election had gone badly yesterday, I might be here now running away from the results. Thank God Keith won. He'll make a fine President of the United States.'

'Yes,' said the man behind the desk. 'We're lucky. If Deutscher had gotten in, we'd have the worst kind of dictatorship. There's an anti-everything man for you, a militarist, anti-Christ, anti-human, anti-intellectual. People called us up, you know, joking but not joking. Said if Deutscher became President they wanted to go live in 1492. Of course it's not our business to conduct Escapes, but to form Safaris. Anyway, Keith's President now. All you got to worry about is——'

'Shooting my dinosaur,' Eckels finished it for him.

'A *Tyrannosaurus rex*. The Thunder Lizard, the damnedest monster in history. Sign this release. Anything happens to you, we're not responsible. Those dinosaurs are hungry.'

Eckels flushed angrily. 'Trying to scare me!'

'Frankly, yes. We don't want anyone going who'll panic at the first shot. Six Safari leaders were killed last year, and a dozen hunters. We're here to give you the damnedest thrill a *real* hunter ever asked for. Travelling you back sixty million years to bag the biggest damned game in all Time. Your personal cheque's still there. Tear it up.'

Mr. Eckels looked at the cheque for a long time. His fingers twitched.

'Good luck,' said the man behind the desk. 'Mr. Travis, he's all yours.'

They moved silently across the room, taking their guns with them, toward the Machine, toward the silver metal and the roaring light.

First a day and then a night and then a day and then a night, then it was day-night-day-night-day. A week, a month, a year, a decade! A.D. 2055. A.D. 2019. 1999! 1957! Gone! The Machine roared.

They put on their oxygen helmets and tested the intercoms.

Eckels swayed on the padded seat, his face pale, his jaw stiff. He felt the trembling in his arms and he looked down and found his hands tight on the new rifle. There were four other men in the Machine. Travis, the Safari Leader, his assistant, Lesperance, and two other hunters, Billings and Kramer. They sat looking at each other, and the years blazed around them.

'Can these guns get a dinosaur cold?' Eckels felt his mouth saying.

'If you hit them right,' said Travis on the helmet radio. 'Some dinosaurs have two brains, one in the head, another far down the spinal column. We stay away from those. That's stretching luck. Put your first two shots into the eyes, if you can, blind them, and go back into the brain.'

The Machine howled. Time was a film run backward. Suns fled and ten million moons fled after them. 'Good God,' said Eckels. 'Every hunter that ever lived would envy us today. This makes Africa seem like Illinois.'

The Machine slowed; its scream fell to a murmur. The Machine stopped.

The sun stopped in the sky.

The fog that had enveloped the Machine blew away and they were in an old time, a very old time indeed, three hunters and two Safari Heads with their blue metal guns across their knees.

'Christ isn't born yet,' said Travis. 'Moses has not gone to the mountain to talk with God. The Pyramids are still in the earth, waiting to be cut out and put up. *Remember* that. Alexander, Caesar, Napoleon, Hitler—none of them exists.'

The men nodded.

'That,'—Mr. Travis pointed—'is the jungle of sixty million two thousand and fifty-five years before President Keith.'

He indicated a metal path that struck off into green wilderness, over steaming swamp, among giant ferns and palms.

'And that,' he said, 'is the Path, laid by Time Safari for your use. It floats six inches above the earth. Doesn't touch so much as one grass blade, flower, or tree. It's an anti-gravity metal. Its purpose is to keep you from touching this world of the past in any way. Stay on the Path. Don't go off it. I repeat. *Don't go off*. For *any* reason! If you fall off, there's a penalty. And don't shoot any animal we don't okay.'

'Why?' asked Eckels.

They sat in the ancient wilderness. Far birds' cries blew on a wind, and the smell of tar and an old salt sea, moist grasses, and flowers the colour of blood.

'We don't want to change the Future. We don't belong here in the Past. The government doesn't *like* us here. We have to pay big graft to keep our franchise. A Time Machine is damn finicky business. Not knowing it, we might kill an important animal, a small bird, a roach, a flower even, thus destroying an important link in a growing species.'

'That's not clear,' said Eckels.

'All right, Travis continued, 'say we accidentally kill one mouse here. That means all the future families of this one particular mouse are destroyed, right?'

'Right.'

'And all the families of the families of the families of that one mouse! With a stamp of your foot, you annihilate first one, then a dozen, then a thousand, a million, a *billion* possible mice!'

'So they're dead,' said Eckels. 'So what?'

'So what?' Travis snorted quietly. 'Well, what about the foxes that'll need those mice to survive? For want of ten mice, a fox dies. For want of ten foxes, a lion starves. For want of a lion, all manner of insects, vultures, infinite billions of life forms are thrown into chaos and destruction. Eventually it all boils down to this: fifty-nine million years later, a cave man, one of a dozen on the *entire world*, goes hunting wild boar or sabre-tooth tiger for food. But you, friend, have *stepped* on all the tigers in that region.

By stepping on *one* single mouse. So the cave man starves. And the cave man, please note, is not just *any* expendable man, no! He is an *entire future nation*. From his loins would have sprung ten sons. From *their* loins one hundred sons, and thus onward to a civilization. Destroy this one man, and you destroy a race, a people, an entire history of life. It is comparable to slaying some of Adam's grandchildren. The stomp of your foot, on one mouse, could start an earthquake, the effects of which could shake our earth and destinies down through Time, to their very foundations. With the death of that one cave man, a billion others yet unborn are throttled in the womb. Perhaps Rome never rises on its seven hills. Perhaps Europe is forever a dark forest, and only Asia waxes healthy and teeming. Step on a mouse and you crush the Pyramids. Step on a mouse and you leave your print, like a Grand Canyon, across Eternity. Queen Elizabeth might never be born, Washington might not cross the Delaware, there might never be a United States at all. So be careful. Stay on the Path. *Never* step off!'

'I see,' said Eckels. 'Then it wouldn't pay for us even to touch the *grass*?'

'Correct. Crushing certain plants could add up infinitesimally. A little error here would multiply in sixty million years, all out of proportion. Of course maybe our theory is wrong. Maybe Time *can't* be changed by us. Or maybe it can be changed only in little subtle ways. A dead mouse here makes an insect imbalance there, a population disproportion later, a bad harvest further on, a depression, mass starvation, and, finally, a change in *social* temperament in far-flung countries. Something much more subtle, like that. Perhaps only a soft breath, a whisper, a hair, pollen on the air, such a slight, slight change that unless you looked close you wouldn't see it. Who knows? Who really can say he knows? We don't know. We're guessing. But until we do know for certain whether our messing around in Time *can* make a big roar or a little rustle in history, we're being damned careful. This Machine, this Path, your clothing and bodies, were sterilised, as you know, before the journey. We wear these oxygen helmets so we can't introduce our bacteria into an ancient atmosphere.'

'How do we know which animals to shoot?'

'They're marked with red paint,' said Travis. 'Today, before our journey, we sent Lesperance here back with the Machine. He came to this particular era and followed certain animals.'

'Studying them?'

'Right,' said Lesperance. 'I track them through their entire existence, noting which of them lives longest. Very few. How many times they mate. Not often. Life's short. When I find one that's going to die when a tree falls on him, or one that drowns in a tar pit, I note the exact hour, minute, and second. I shoot a paint bomb. It leaves a red patch on his side. We can't miss it. Then I correlate our arrival in the Past so that we meet the Monster not more than two minutes before he would have died anyway. This way, we kill only animals with no future, that are never going to mate again. You see how *careful* we are?'

'But if you came back this morning in Time,' said Eckels eagerly, 'you must've bumped into *us*, our Safari! How did it turn out? Was it successful? Did all of us get through—alive?'

Travis and Lesperance gave each other a look.

'That'd be a paradox,' said the latter. 'Time doesn't permit that sort of mess—a man meeting himself. When such occasions threaten, Time steps aside. Like an airplane hitting an air pocket. You felt the Machine jump just before we stopped? That was us passing ourselves on the way back to the Future. We saw nothing. There's no way of telling *if* this expedition was a success, *if we* got our monster, or whether all of us—meaning *you*, Mr. Eckels—got out alive.'

Eckels smiled palely.

'Cut that,' said Travis sharply. 'Everyone on his feet!'

They were ready to leave the Machine.

The jungle was high and the jungle was broad and the jungle was the entire world forever and forever. Sounds like music and sounds like flying tents filled the sky, and those were pterodactyls soaring with cavernous grey wings, gigantic bats out of delirium and a night fever. Eckels, balanced on the narrow Path, aimed his rifle playfully.

'Stop that!' said Travis. 'Don't even aim for fun, damn it! If your guns should go off——'

Eckels flushed. 'Where's our *Tyrannosaurus ?*'

Lesperance checked his wrist watch. 'Up ahead. We'll bisect his trail in sixty seconds. Look for the red paint, for Christ's sake. Don't shoot till we give the word. Stay on the Path. *Stay on the Path !*'

They moved forward in the wind of morning.

'Strange,' murmured Eckels. 'Up ahead, sixty million years, Election Day over. Keith made President. Everyone celebrating. And here we are, a million years lost, and they don't exist. The things we worried about for months, a lifetime, not even born or thought about yet.'

'Safety catches off, everyone!' ordered Travis. 'You, first shot, Eckels. Second, Billings. Third, Kramer.'

'I've hunted tiger, wild boar, buffalo, elephant, but Jesus, this is *it*,' said Eckels. 'I'm shaking like a kid.'

'Ah,' said Travis.

Everyone stopped.

Travis raised his hand. 'Ahead,' he whispered. 'In the mist. There he is. There's His Royal Majesty now.'

The jungle was wide and full of twitterings, rustlings, murmurs, and sighs.

Suddenly it all ceased, as if someone had shut a door.

Silence.

A sound of thunder.

Out of the mist, one hundred yards away, came *Tyrannosaurus rex*.

'Jesus God,' whispered Eckels.

'Sh!'

It came on great oiled, resilient, striding legs. It towered thirty feet above half of the trees, a great evil god, folding its delicate watchmaker's claws close to its oily reptilian chest. Each lower leg was a piston, a thousand pounds of white bone, sunk in thick ropes of muscle, sheathed over in a gleam of pebbled skin like the mail of a terrible warrior. Each thigh was a ton of meat, ivory, and steel mesh. And from the great breathing cage of the upper body those two delicate arms dangled out front, arms with hands which might pick up and examine men like toys, while the snake neck coiled. And the head itself, a ton of sculptured stone, lifted easily upon the sky. Its mouth gaped, exposing a fence of teeth like daggers. Its eyes rolled, ostrich eggs, empty of all expression save hunger. It closed its mouth in a death grin. It ran, its pelvic bones crushing aside trees and bushes, its taloned feet clawing damp earth, leaving prints six inches deep wherever it settled its weight. It ran with a gliding ballet step, far too poised and balanced for its ten tons. It moved into a sunlit arena warily, its beautifully reptile hands feeling the air.

'My God!' Eckels twitched his mouth. 'It could reach up and grab the moon.'

'Sh!' Travis jerked angrily. 'He hasn't seen us yet.'

'It can't be killed.' Eckels pronounced this verdict quietly, as if there could be no argument. He had weighed the evidence and this was his considered opinion. The rifle in his hands seemed a cap gun. 'We were fools to come. This is impossible.'

'Shut up!' hissed Travis.

'Nightmare.'

'Turn around,' commanded Travis. 'Walk quietly to the Machine. We'll remit one half your fee.'

'I didn't realise it would be this *big*,' said Eckels. 'I miscalculated, that's all. And now I want out.'

'It *sees* us!'

'There's the red paint on its chest!'

The Thunder Lizard raised itself. Its armoured flesh glittered like a thousand green coins. The coins, crusted with slime, steamed. In the slime, tiny insects wriggled, so that the entire body seemed to twitch and undulate, even while the monster itself did not move. It exhaled. The stink of raw flesh blew down the wilderness.

'Get me out of here,' said Eckels. 'It was never like this before. I was always sure I'd come through alive. I had good guides, good safaris, and safety. This time, I figured wrong. I've met my match and admit it. This is too much for me to get hold of.'

'Don't run,' said Lesperance. 'Turn around. Hide in the Machine.'

'Yes,' Eckels seemed to be numb. He looked at his feet as if trying to make them move. He gave a grunt of helplessness.

'Eckels!'

He took a few steps, blinking, shuffling.

'Not *that* way!'

The Monster, at the first motion, lunged forward with a terrible scream. It covered one hundred yards in four seconds. The rifles jerked up and blazed fire. A windstorm from the beast's mouth engulfed them in the stench of slime and old blood. The Monster roared, teeth glittering with sun.

Eckels, not looking back, walked blindly to the edge of the Path, his gun limp in his arms, stepped off the Path, and walked, not knowing it, in the jungle. His feet sank into green moss. His legs moved him, and he felt alone and remote from the events behind.

The rifles cracked again. Their sound was lost in shriek and lizard thunder. The great lever of the reptile's tail swung up, lashed sideways. Trees exploded in clouds of leaf and branch. The

Monster twitched its jeweller's hands down to fondle at the men, to twist them in half, to crush them like berries, to cram them into its teeth and its screaming throat. Its boulder-stone eyes levelled with the men. They saw themselves mirrored. They fired at the metallic eyelids and the blazing black iris.

Like a stone idol, like a mountain avalanche, *Tyrannosaurus* fell. Thundering, it clutched trees, pulled them with it. It wrenched and tore the metal Path. The men flung themselves back and away. The body hit, ten tons of cold flesh and stone. The guns fired. The Monster lashed its armoured tail, twitched its snake jaws, and lay still. A fount of blood spurted from its throat. Somewhere inside, a sac of fluids burst. Sickening gushes drenched the hunters. They stood, red and glistening.

The thunder faded.

The jungle was silent. After the avalanche, a green peace. After the nightmare, morning.

Billings and Kramer sat on the pathway and threw up. Travis and Lesperance stood with smoking rifles, cursing steadily.

In the Time Machine, on his face, Eckels lay shivering. He had found his way back to the Path, climbed into the Machine.

Travis came walking, glanced at Eckels, took cotton gauze from a metal box, and returned to the others, who were sitting on the Path.

'Clean up.'

They wiped the blood from their helmets. They began to curse too. The Monster lay, a hill of solid flesh. Within, you could hear the sighs and murmurs as the furthest chambers of it died, the organs malfunctioning, liquids running a final instant from pocket to sac to spleen, everything shutting off, closing up forever. It was like standing by a wrecked locomotive or a steam shovel at quitting time, all valves being released or levered tight. Bones cracked; the tonnage of its own flesh, off balance, dead weight, snapped the delicate forearms, caught underneath. The meat settled, quivering.

Another cracking sound. Overhead, a gigantic tree branch broke from its heavy mooring, fell. It crashed upon the dead beast with finality.

'There.' Lesperance checked his watch. 'Right on time. That's the giant tree that was scheduled to fall and kill this animal originally.' He glanced at the two hunters. 'You want the trophy picture?'

'What?'

'We can't take a trophy back to the Future. The body has to stay right here where it would have died originally, so the insects, birds, and bacteria can get at it, as they were intended to. Everything in balance. The body stays. But we *can* take a picture of you standing near it.'

The two men tried to think, but gave up, shaking their heads.

They let themselves be led along the metal Path. They sank wearily into the Machine cushions. They gazed back at the ruined

Monster, the stagnating mound, where already strange reptilian birds and golden insects were busy at the steaming armour.

A sound on the floor of the Time Machine stiffened them. Eckels sat there, shivering.

'I'm sorry,' he said at last.

'Get up!' cried Travis.

Eckels got up.

'Go out on that Path alone,' said Travis. He had his rifle pointed. 'You're not coming back in the Machine. We're leaving you here!'

Lesperance seized Travis's arm. 'Wait——'

'Stay out of this!' Travis shook his hand away. 'This son of a bitch nearly killed us. But it isn't *that* so much. Hell, no. It's his *shoes!* Look at them! He ran off the Path. My God, that *ruins* us! Christ knows how much we'll forfeit! Tens of thousands of dollars of insurance! We guarantee no one leaves the Path. He left it. Oh, the damn fool! I'll have to report to the government. They might revoke our licence to travel. God knows *what* he's done to Time, to History!'

'Take it easy, all he did was kick up some dirt.'

'How do we *know?*' cried Travis. 'We don't know anything! It's a damn mystery! Get out here, Eckels!'

Eckels fumbled his shirt. 'I'll pay anything. A hundred thousand dollars!'

Travis glared at Eckel's cheque book and spat. 'Go out there. The Monster's next to the Path. Stick your arms up to your elbows in his mouth. Then you can come back with us.'

'That's unreasonable!'

'The Monster's dead, you yellow bastard. The bullets! The bullets can't be left behind. They don't belong in the Past; they might change something. Here's my knife. Dig them out!'

The jungle was alive again, full of the old tremorings and bird cries. Eckels turned slowly to regard that primeval garbage dump, that hill of nightmares and terror. After a long time, like a sleep-walker, he shuffled out along the Path.

He returned, shuddering, five minutes later, his arms soaked and red to the elbows. He held out his hands. Each held a number of steel bullets. Then he fell. He lay where he fell, not moving.

'You didn't have to make him do that,' said Lesperance.

'Didn't I? It's too early to tell.' Travis nudged the still body. 'He'll live. Next time he won't go hunting game like this. Okay.' He jerked his thumb wearily at Lesperance. 'Switch on. Let's go home.'

1492. 1776. 1812.

They cleaned their hands and faces. They changed their caking shirts and pants. Eckels was up and around again, not speaking. Travis glared at him for a full ten minutes.

'Don't look at me,' cried Eckels. 'I haven't done anything.'

'Who can tell?'

'Just ran off the Path, that's all, a little mud on my shoes—what do you want me to do—get down and pray?'

'We might need it. I'm warning you, Eckels, I might kill you yet. I've got my gun ready.'

'I'm innocent. I've done nothing!'

1999. 2000. 2055.

The Machine stopped.

'Get out,' said Travis.

The room was there as they had left it. But not the same as they had left it. The same man sat behind the same desk. But the same man did not quite sit behind the same desk.

Travis looked around swiftly. 'Everything okay here?' he snapped.

'Fine. Welcome home!'

Travis did not relax. He seemed to be looking at the very atoms of the air itself, at the way the sun poured through the one high window.

'Okay, Eckels, get out. Don't ever come back.'

Eckels could not move.

'You heard me,' said Travis. 'What're you *staring* at ?'

Eckels stood smelling of the air, and there was a thing to the air, a chemical taint so subtle, so slight, that only a faint cry of his sublimal senses warned him it was there. The colours, white, grey, blue, orange, in the wall, in the furniture, in the sky beyond the window, were . . . were . . . And there was a *feel*. His flesh twitched. His hands twitched. He stood drinking the oddness with the pores of his body. Somewhere, someone must have been screaming one of those whistles that only a dog can hear. His body screamed silence in return. Beyond this room, beyond this wall, beyond this man who was not quite the same man seated at this desk that was not quite the same desk . . . lay an entire world of streets and people. What sort of world it was now, there was no telling. He could feel them moving there, beyond the walls, almost, like so many chess pieces blown in a dry wind . . . .

But the immediate thing was the sign painted on the office wall, the same sign he had read earlier today on first entering.

Somehow, the sign had changed:

> TYME SEFARI INC.
>
> SEFARIS TU ANY YEER EN THE PAST.
>
> YU NAIM THE ANIMALL.
>
> WEE TAEK YU THAIR.
>
> YU SHOOT ITT.

Eckels felt himself fall into a chair. He fumbled crazily at the thick slime on his boots. He held up a clod of dirt, trembling. 'No, it *can't* be. Not a *little* thing like that. No!'

Embedded in the mud, glistening green and gold and black, was a butterfly, very beautiful, and very dead.

'Not a little thing like *that* ! Not a butterfly!' cried Eckels.

It fell to the floor, an exquisite thing, a small thing that could upset balances and knock down a line of small dominoes and then big dominoes and then gigantic dominoes, all down the years across Time. Eckels' mind whirled. It *couldn't* change things. Killing one butterfly couldn't be *that* important! Could it?

His face was cold. His mouth trembled, asking: 'Who—who won the presidential election yesterday?'

The man behind the desk laughed. 'You joking? You know damn well. Deutscher, of course! Who else? Not that damn weakling Keith. We got an iron man now, a man with guts, by God!' The official stopped. 'What's wrong?'

Eckels moaned. He dropped to his knees. He scrabbled at the golden butterfly with shaking fingers. 'Can't we,' he pleaded to the world, to himself, to the officials, to the Machine, 'can't we take it *back*, can't we *make* it alive again? Can't we start over? Can't we——'

He did not move. Eyes shut, he waited, shivering. He heard Travis breathe loud in the room; he heard Travis shift his rifle, click the safety catch, and raise the weapon.

There was a sound of thunder.

RAY BRADBURY

Guy de Maupassant

Guy de Maupassant was born in 1850 in the Norman château of Miromesnil. The parting of his parents when he was eleven made a lasting impression on him and strongly influenced his writing. Following the break-up of the marriage, his mother turned for advice to her friend Gustave Flaubert, the well-known French novelist, who later played a leading part in Maupassant's literary career. After a short spell as a soldier in the Franco-German War, Maupassant was employed from 1872 to 1880 as a clerk in the Civil Service. During this time he practised the craft of writing and regularly took his work to Flaubert for comment and correction. In 1880 he had an audacious tale about the Franco-German War, 'Boule de Suif', published in a composite volume of short stories. This brought him immediate success; he was able to earn his living by writing and became one of the most popular and highly paid of French authors. Towards the end of his life he became insane; he died in Paris in 1893.

He is best known for his numerous short stories, which often exposed the pretentiousness of the middle classes and the lower reaches of bureaucracy, e.g. 'The Necklace' (*Storytellers 1*); others dealt with the cunning and traditional meanness of Norman peasants, e.g. 'The Devil' (*Storytellers 2*); episodes in the Franco-German War also provided him with a rich source of material. His style was detached; the tone was cynical; and the stories themselves often had a surprise ending. His superb craftsmanship, verging on slickness, has caused him to be described as 'the virtual inventor of the commercial short story'. 'En Famille', 'The Rendezvous' and 'The Umbrella' are three other well-known and characteristic stories.

The Necklace

SHE was one of those attractive pretty girls, born by a freak of fortune in a lower-middle-class family. She had no dowry, no expectations, no way of getting known, appreciated, loved and married by some wealthy gentleman of good family. And she allowed herself to be married to a junior clerk in the Ministry of Public Instruction.

She dressed plainly, having no money to spend on herself. But she was as unhappy as if she had known better days. Women have no sense of caste or breeding, their beauty, their grace, and their charm taking the place of birth and family. Their natural refinement, their instinctive delicacy and adaptability are their only passport to society, and these qualities enable daughters of the people to compete with ladies of gentle birth.

She always had a sense of frustration, feeling herself born for all the refinements and luxuries of life. She hated the bareness of her flat, the shabbiness of the walls, the worn upholstery of the chairs, and the ugliness of the curtains. All these things, which another woman of her class would not even have noticed, were pain and grief to her. The sight of the little Breton maid doing her simple house-work aroused in her passionate regrets and hopeless dreams. She imagined hushed ante-rooms hung with oriental fabrics and lit by tall bronze candelabra, with two impressive footmen in knee-breeches dozing in great armchairs, made drowsy by the heat of radiators. She imagined vast drawing-rooms, upholstered in antique silk, splendid pieces of furniture littered with priceless curios, and dainty scented boudoirs, designed for tea-time conversation with intimate friends and much-sought-after society gentlemen, whose attentions every woman envies and desires.

When she sat down to dinner at the round table covered with a three-days-old cloth opposite her husband, who took the lid off the casserole with the delighted exclamation: 'Ah! hot-pot again! How lovely! It's the best dish in the world!' she was dreaming of luxurious dinners with gleaming silver and tapestries peopling the walls with classical figures and exotic birds in a fairy forest; she dreamt of exquisite dishes served on valuable china and whispered compliments listened to with a sphinx-like smile, while toying with the pink flesh of a trout or the wing of a hazel-hen.

She had a rich friend who had been with her at a convent school, but she did not like going to see her now, the contrast was so painful when she went home. She spent whole days in tears; misery, regrets, hopeless longings caused her such bitter distress.

One evening her husband came home with a broad smile on his face and a large envelope in his hand: 'Look!' he cried. 'Here's something for you, dear!'

She tore open the envelope eagerly and pulled out a printed card with the words: 'The Minister of Public Instruction and Mme Georges Ramponneau request the honour of the company of M. and Mme Loisel at the Ministry on the evening of Monday, January 18th.'

Instead of being delighted as her husband had hoped, she threw the invitation pettishly down on the table, murmuring:

'What's the good of this to me?'

'But I thought you'd be pleased, dear! You never go out and this is an occasion, a great occasion. I had the greatest difficulty to get the invitation. Everybody wants one; it's very select and

junior clerks don't often get asked. The whole official world will be there.'

She looked at him crossly and declared impatiently: 'What do you think I'm to wear?'

He hadn't thought of that and stuttered: 'Why! the frock you wear for the theatre. I think it's charming.!'

He stopped in astonished bewilderment when he saw his wife was crying. Two great tears were running slowly down from the corners of her eyes to the corners of her mouth; he stammered: 'What's the matter? What's the matter?'

But with a great effort she had controlled her disappointment and replied quietly, drying her wet cheeks: 'Oh! Nothing! Only not having anything to wear I can't go to the party. Pass on the invitation to some colleague whose wife is better dressed than I.'

'Look here, Mathilde! How much would a suitable frock cost, something quite simple that would be useful on other occasions later on?'

She thought for a few seconds, doing a sum and also wondering how much she could ask for without inviting an immediate refusal and an outraged exclamation from the close-fisted clerk. At last with some hesitation she replied: 'I don't know exactly but I think I could manage on four hundred francs.'

He went slightly pale, for this was just the amount he had put by to get a gun so that he could enjoy some shooting the following summer on the Nanterre plain with some friends who went out lark-shooting on Sundays. But he said: 'Right! I'll give you four hundred francs, but try to get a really nice frock.'

The date of the party was approaching and Mme Loisel seemed depressed and worried, though her dress was ready. One evening her husband said to her: 'What's the matter? The last three days you've not been yourself.'

She replied: 'It's rotten not to have a piece of jewellery, not a stone of any kind to wear. I shall look poverty-stricken. I'd rather not go the the party.'

He answered: 'But you can wear some real flowers. That's very smart this year. For ten francs you could get two or three magnificent roses.'

She was not impressed. 'No, there's nothing more humiliating than to look poor in a crowd of wealthy women.'

But her husband suddenly cried: 'What a fool you are! Go to your friend, Mme Forestier, and ask her to lend you some of her jewellery. You know her well enough to do that.'

She uttered a joyful cry: 'That's a good idea! I'd never thought of it!'

Next day she went to her friend's house and explained her dilemma.

Mme Forestier went to a glass-fronted wardrobe, took out

a large casket, brought it over, opened it, and said to Mme Loisel:

'Take what you like, my dear!'

First she looked at bracelets, then a pearl collar, then a Venetian cross in gold and stones, a lovely piece of work. She tried the various ornaments in front of the glass, unable to make up her mind to take them off and put them back; she kept asking: 'Haven't you got anything else?'

'Yes, go on looking; I don't know what you would like.'

Suddenly she found a black satin case containing a magnificent diamond necklace, and she wanted it so desperately that her heart began to thump. Her hands were shaking as she picked it up. She put it round her throat over her high blouse and stood in ecstasy before her reflection in the glass. Then she asked hesitantly, her anxiety showing in her voice: 'Could you lend me that, just that, nothing else?'

'But of course!'

She threw her arms round her friend's neck and kissed her wildly, and hurried home with her treasure.

The day of the party arrived. Mme Loisel had a triumph. She was the prettiest woman in the room, elegant, graceful, smiling, in the seventh heaven of happiness. All the men looked at her, asked who she was, and wanted to be introduced. All the private secretaries wanted to dance with her. The Minister himself noticed her.

She danced with inspired abandon, intoxicated with delight, thinking of nothing in the triumph of her beauty and the glory of her success; she was wrapped in a cloud of happiness, the result of all the compliments, all the admiration, all these awakened desires, that wonderful success so dear to every woman's heart.

She left about four in the morning. Her husband had been dozing since midnight in a small, empty drawing-room with three other gentlemen, whose wives were also enjoying themselves.

He threw over her shoulders the wraps he had brought for going home, her simple everyday coat, whose plainness clashed with the smartness of her ball dress. She was conscious of this and wanted to hurry away, so as not to be noticed by the ladies who were putting on expensive fur wraps.

Loisel tried to stop her: 'Wait a minute! You'll catch cold outside. I'll call a cab.'

But she would not listen and ran down the stairs. When they got into the street they could not find a cab and began to hunt for one, shouting to the drivers they saw passing in the distance. In despair they went down towards the Seine, shivering. At last, on the Embankment they found one of those old broughams that ply by night and are only seen in Paris after dark, as if ashamed of their shabbiness in the daytime. It took them back to their house in the Rue des Martyrs and they went sadly up to their flat. For her this was the end; and he was remembering that he had got to be at the office at ten o'clock.

She took off the wraps she had put round her shoulders, standing in front of the glass to see herself once more in all her glory. But suddenly she uttered a cry; the diamond necklace was no longer round her neck. Her husband, already half undressed, asked: 'What's the matter?'

She turned to him in a panic: 'Mme Forestier's necklace has gone!'

He stood up, dumbfounded: 'What? What do you mean? It's impossible!'

They searched in the folds of her dress, in the folds of her cloak in the pockets, everywhere; they could not find it. He asked: 'Are you sure you had it on when you left the ball?'

'Yes, I fingered it in the hall at the Ministry.'

'But, if you had lost it in the street, we should have heard it drop. It must be in the cab.'

'Yes, it probably is. Did you take the number?'

'No! And you didn't notice it, I suppose?'

'No!'

They looked at each other, utterly crushed. Finally Loisel dressed again: 'I'll go back along the way we walked and see if I can find it.'

He went out and she remained in her evening dress, without the strength even to go to bed, collapsed on a chair, without a fire, her mind a blank.

Her husband returned about seven, having found nothing. He went to the police station, to the papers to offer a reward, to the cab companies, in fact anywhere that gave a flicker of hope.

She waited all day in the same state of dismay at this appalling catastrophe. Loisel came back in the evening, his face pale and lined; he had discovered nothing.

'You must write to your friend,' he said, 'and say you have

broken the clasp of the necklace and are getting it mended. That will give us time to turn round.'

So she wrote at his dictation. After a week they had lost all hope and Loisel, who had aged five years, declared: 'We must do something about replacing it.'

Next day they took the case which had contained the necklace to the jeweller whose name was in it. He looked up his books: 'I did not sell the jewel, Madame; I must only have supplied the case.'

They went from jeweller to jeweller, looking for a necklace like the other, trying to remember exactly what it was like, both of them sick with worry and anxiety.

At last in the Palais-Royal they found a diamond necklace just like the one lost. Its price was forty thousand francs, but they could have it for thirty-six thousand.

So they asked the jeweller to keep it for three days. They made it a condition that he should take it back for thirty-four thousand if the first was found before the end of February.

Loisel had got eighteen thousand francs which his father had left him; he would borrow the rest.

He borrowed one thousand francs from one, five hundred from another, one hundred here, sixty there. He gave I.O.U.s and notes of hand on ruinous terms, going to the Jews and money-lenders of every kind. He mortgaged the whole of the rest of his life, risked his signature on bills without knowing if he would ever be able to honour it; he was tormented with anxiety about the future, with the thought of the crushing poverty about to descend upon him and the prospect of physical privations and mental agony. Then he went and collected the necklace, putting down the thirty-six thousand francs on the jeweller's counter.

When Mme Loisel took the necklace back to Mme Forestier, the latter said rather coldly: 'You ought to have brought it back sooner; I might have wanted it.'

She did not open the case, as her friend had feared she might. If she had detected the replacement what would she have thought? What would she have said? Would she have considered her a thief?

Now Mme Loisel learnt to know the grim life of the very poor. However, she faced the position with heroic courage. This ghastly debt must be paid and she would pay it. They got rid of the maid; they gave up the flat and took an attic under the tiles. She did all the heavy work of the house as well as the hateful kitchen jobs. She washed up, ruining her pink nails on the coarse crockery and the bottoms of the saucepans. She washed the dirty linen and shirts and the kitchen cloths and dried them on a line. She carried the rubbish down to the street every morning and brought up the water, stopping on every floor to get her breath. And dressed as a woman of the people, she went to the fruiterer, the grocer and the butcher with her basket on her arm, bargaining in spite of their rudeness and fighting for every penny of her miserable pittance.

Every month some notes of hand had to be paid off and others renewed to gain time. Her husband worked in the evening keeping a tradesman's books and often at night he did copying at twenty-five centimes a page. This life went on for ten years.

After ten years they had paid everything back, including the interest and the accumulated compound interest.

Mme Loisel now looked an old woman. She had become the strong, tough, coarse woman we find in the homes of the poor. Her hair was neglected, her skirt was askew, her hands were red and her voice loud: she even scrubbed the floors. But sometimes, when her husband was at the office, she would sit down near the window and dream of that evening long ago, the ball at which she had been such a success.

What would have happened to her if she had not lost the necklace? Who can say? Life is such a strange thing with its changes and chances. Such a little thing can make or mar it!

One Sunday, when she had gone for a stroll in the Champs-Élysees as a change from the week's grind, she suddenly saw a lady taking a child for a walk. It was Mme Forestier, still young, still beautiful, still attractive.

Mme Loisel felt a wave of emotion. Should she speak to her? Yes, she would. Now that she had paid, she would tell her everything. Why not?

She went up to her: 'Good morning, Jeanne!'

The other woman did not recognise her, surprised at being addressed in this familiar fashion by a common woman; she stammered: 'But, Madame . . . I don't know you . . . there must be some mistake.'

'No! I'm Mathilde Loisel!'

Her friend exclaimed: 'Oh! Poor Mathilde, how you've changed!'

'Yes, I've had a pretty grim time since I saw you last, with lots of trouble—and it was all your fault!'

'My fault? What do you mean?'

'You remember that diamond necklace you lent me to go to the party at the Ministry?'

'Yes, what about it?'

'Well! I lost it!'

'What! But you brought it back to me.'

'I brought you back another exactly like it; and for ten years we've been paying for it. You'll realise it hasn't been easy, for we had no money of our own. Well, now it's all over and I'm jolly glad!'

Mme Forestier had stopped: 'You say you bought a diamond necklace to replace mine?'

'Yes! And you never spotted it, did you? They were as like as two peas.'

And she smiled with simple proud pleasure.

Mme Forestier, deeply moved, took both her hands: 'Oh! my poor Mathilde! But mine was only paste, not worth more than five hundred francs at most.'   MAUPASSANT

John Steinbeck

John Steinbeck was born in 1902 in Salinas, California, U.S.A. He was educated at Salinas High School and studied science at Stanford University, after which he had a variety of jobs, most of them involving manual labour. He took his native state of California as the background for most of his early short stories and novels. His first success, *Tortilla Flat* (1935)—which enabled him to become a full-time writer—was a picaresque story of Monterey *paisanas;* this was followed by *In Dubious Battle*, a grim novel about a labour strike. His concern with the depressed economic classes of the United States led him to write *The Grapes of Wrath*, an epic story of a family from the dust bowl of the West who seek work in the 'promised land' of California. This masterpiece of contemporary literature provoked much-needed reform and gained Steinbeck the Pulitzer Prize of 1940. He acted as a war correspondent overseas in 1943 and between then and his death in 1969 continued to produce a wide variety of stories. He was awarded the Nobel Prize for Literature in 1962.

Steinbeck's writing has great power: his descriptions, particularly of the landscape and of manual workers, show tremendous understanding; the pace of his stories never flags; the style is rich yet clear. Many critics, however, have called attention to over-simplification and sentimentality in his work. Traces of these faults can be detected in 'The Leader of the People' (*Storytellers 1*) and 'Breakfast' (*Storytellers 2*), but his talents are, nevertheless, much more obvious than his defects; both stories are taken from *The Long Valley* (1938). Other books that you may enjoy include *Of Mice and Men*—a story about two farm labourers, one of great strength and weak mind, who is both exploited and protected by the other; *The Pearl; Cannery Row; The Wayward Bus;* and *The Short Reign of Pippin IV*.

The Leader of the People

ON Saturday afternoon Billy Buck, the ranch-hand, raked together the last of the old year's haystack and pitched small forkfuls over the wire fence to a few mildly interested cattle. High in the air small clouds like puffs of cannon smoke were driven eastward by the March wind. The wind could be heard whishing in the brush on the ridge crests, but no breath of it penetrated down into the ranch-cup.

The little boy, Jody, emerged from the house eating a thick piece of buttered bread. He saw Billy working on the last of the haystack. Jody tramped down scuffing his shoes in a way he had been told was destructive to good shoe-leather. A flock of white pigeons flew out of the black cypress tree as Jody passed, and circled the tree and landed again. A half-grown tortoise-shell cat leaped from the bunkhouse porch, galloped on stiff legs across the road, whirled and galloped back again. Jody picked up a stone to help the game along, but he was too late, for the cat was under the porch before the stone could be discharged. He threw the stone into the cypress tree and started the white pigeons on another whirling flight.

Arriving at the used-up haystack, the boy leaned against the barbed wire fence. 'Will that be all of it, do you think?' he asked.

The middle-aged ranch-hand stopped his careful raking and stuck his fork into the ground. He took off his black hat and smoothed down his hair. 'Nothing left of it that isn't soggy from

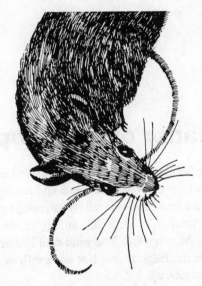

ground moisture,' he said. He replaced his hat and rubbed his dry leathery hands together.

'Ought to be plenty mice,' Jody suggested.

'Lousy with them,' said Billy. 'Just crawling with mice.'

'Well, maybe, when you get all through, I could call the dogs and hunt the mice.'

'Sure, I guess you could,' said Billy Buck. He lifted a forkful of the damp ground-hay and threw it into the air. Instantly three mice leaped out and burrowed frantically under the hay again.

Jody sighed with satisfaction. Those plump, sleek, arrogant mice were doomed. For eight months they had lived and multiplied in the haystack. They had been immune from cats, from traps, from poison and from Jody. They had grown smug in their security, overbearing and fat. Now the time of disaster had come; they would not survive another day.

Billy looked up at the top of the hills that surrounded the ranch. 'Maybe you better ask your father before you do it,' he suggested.

'Well, where is he? I'll ask him now.'

'He rode up to the ridge ranch after dinner. He'll be back pretty soon.'

Jody slumped against the fence post. 'I don't think he'd care.'

As Billy went back to his work he said ominously, 'You'd better ask him anyway. You know how he is.'

Jody did know. His father, Carl Tiflin, insisted upon giving permission for anything that was done on the ranch, whether it was important or not. Jody sagged farther against the post until he was sitting on the ground. He looked up at the little puffs of wind-driven cloud. 'Is it like to rain, Billy?'

'It might. The wind's good for it, but not strong enough.'

'Well, I hope it don't rain until after I kill those damn mice.' He looked over his shoulder to see whether Billy had noticed the mature profanity. Billy worked on without comment.

Jody turned back and looked at the side-hill where the road from the outside world came down. The hill was washed with lean March sunshine. Silver thistles, blue lupins and a few poppies bloomed among the sage bushes. Halfway up the hill Jody could see Doubletree Mutt, the black dog, digging in a squirrel hole. He paddled for a while and then paused to kick bursts of dirt out between his hind legs, and he dug with an earnestness which belied the knowledge he must have had that no dog had ever caught a squirrel by digging in a hole.

Suddenly, while Jody watched, the black dog stiffened, and backed out of the hole and looked up the hill toward the cleft in the ridge where the road came through. Jody looked up too. For a moment Carl Tiflin on horseback stood out against the pale sky and then he moved down the road towards the house. He carried something white in his hand.

The boy started to his feet. 'He's got a letter,' Jody cried. He trotted away toward the ranch house, for the letter would probably be read aloud and he wanted to be there. He reached the house before his father did, and ran in. He heard Carl dismount from his creaking saddle and slap the horse on the side to send it to the barn where Billy would unsaddle it and turn it out.

Jody ran into the kitchen. 'We got a letter!' he cried.

His mother looked up from a pan of beans. 'Who has?'

'Father has. I saw it in his hand.'

Carl strode into the kitchen then, and Jody's mother asked, 'Who's the letter from, Carl?'

He frowned quickly. 'How did you know there was a letter?'

She nodded her head in the boy's direction. 'Big-Britches Jody told me.'

Jody was embarrassed.

His father looked down at him contemptuously. 'He *is* getting to be a Big-Britches,' Carl said. 'He's minding everybody's business but his own. Got his big nose into everything.'

Mrs. Tiflin relented a little. 'Well, he hasn't enough to keep him busy. Who's the letter from?'

Carl still frowned on Jody. 'I'll keep him busy if he isn't careful.' He held out a sealed letter. 'I guess it's from your father.'

Mrs. Tiflin took a hairpin from her head and slit open the flap. Her lips pursed judiciously. Jody saw her eyes snap back and forth over the lines. 'He says,' she translated, 'he says he's going to drive out Saturday to stay for a little while. Why, this is Saturday. The letter must have been delayed.' She looked at the postmark. 'This was mailed day before yesterday. It should have been here yesterday.' She looked up questioningly at her husband and then her face darkened angrily. 'Now what have you got that look on you for? He doesn't come often.'

Carl turned his eyes away from her anger. He could be stern with her most of the time, but when occasionally her temper arose, he could not combat it.

'What's the matter with you?' she demanded again.

In his explanation there was a tone of apology Jody himself

might have used. 'It's just that he talks,' Carl said lamely. 'Just talks.'

'Well, what of it ? You talk yourself.'

'Sure I do. But your father only talks about one thing.'

'Indians!' Jody broke in excitedly. 'Indians and crossing the plains!'

Carl turned fiercely on him. 'You get out, Mr. Big-Britches! Go on, now! Get out!'

Jody went miserably out the back door and closed the screen with elaborate quietness. Under the kitchen window his shamed, downcast eyes fell upon a curiously shaped stone, a stone of such fascination that he squatted down and picked it up and turned it over in his hands.

The voices came clearly to him through the open kitchen window. 'Jody's damn well right,' he heard his father say. 'Just Indians and crossing the plains. I've heard that story about how the horses got driven off about a thousand times. He just goes on and on, and he never changes a word in the thing he tells.'

When Mrs. Teflin answered her tone was so changed that Jody, outside the window, looked up from his study of the stone. Her voice had become soft and explanatory. Jody knew how her face would have changed to match the tone. She said quietly, 'Look at it this way, Carl. That was the big thing in my father's life. He led a wagon train clear across the plains to the coast, and when it was finished, his life was done. It was a big thing to do, but it didn't last long enough. Look!' she continued, 'it's as though he was born to do that, and after he finished it, there wasn't anything more for him to do but think about it and talk about it. If there'd been any farther west to go, he'd have gone. He's told me so himself. But at last there was the ocean. He lives right by the ocean where he had to stop.'

She had caught Carl, caught him and entangled him in her soft tone.

'I've seen him,' he agreed quietly. 'He goes down and stares off west over the ocean.' His voice sharpened a little. 'And then he goes up to the Horseshoe Club in Pacific Grove, and he tells people how the Indians drove off the horses.'

She tried to catch him again. 'Well, it's everything to him. You might be patient with him and pretend to listen.'

Carl turned impatiently away. 'Well, if it gets too bad, I can always go down to the bunkhouse and sit with Billy,' he said

irritably. He walked through the house and slammed the front door after him.

Jody ran to his chores. He dumped the grain to the chickens without chasing any of them. He gathered the eggs from the nests. He trotted into the house with the wood and interlaced it so carefully in the wood-box that two armloads seemed to fill it to overflowing.

His mother had finished the beans by now. She stirred up the fire and brushed off the stove-top with a turkey wing. Jody peered cautiously at her to see whether any rancor towards him remained. 'Is he coming today?' Jody asked.

'That's what his letter said.'

'Maybe I better walk up the road to meet him.'

Mrs. Tiflin clanged the stove-lid shut. 'That would be nice,' she said. 'He'd probably like to be met.'

'I guess I'll do it then.'

Outside, Jody whistled shrilly to the dogs. 'Come on up the hill,' he commanded. The two dogs waved their tails and ran ahead. Along the roadside the sage had tender new tips. Jody tore off some pieces and rubbed them on his hands until the air was filled with the sharp wild smell. With a rush the dogs leaped from the road and yapped into the brush after a rabbit. That was the last Jody saw of them, for when they failed to catch the rabbit, they went back home.

Jody plodded on up the hill toward the ridge top. When he reached the little cleft where the road came through, the afternoon wind struck him and blew up his hair and ruffled his shirt. He looked down on the little hills and ridges below and then out at the huge green Salinas Valley. He could see the white town of Salinas far out in the flat and the flash of its windows under the waning sun. Directly below him, in an oak tree, a crow congress had convened. The tree was black with crows all cawing at once.

Then Jody's eyes followed the wagon road down from the ridge where he stood, and lost it behind a hill, and picked it up again on the other side. On that distant stretch he saw a cart slowly pulled by a bay horse. It disappeared behind the hill. Jody sat down on the ground and watched the place where the cart would reappear again. The wind sang on the hilltops and the puff-ball clouds hurried eastward.

Then the cart came into sight and stopped. A man dressed in black dismounted from the seat and walked to the horse's head.

Although it was so far away, Jody knew he had unhooked the check-rein, for the horse's head dropped forward. The horse moved on, and the man walked slowly up the hill beside it. Jody gave a glad cry and ran down the road toward them. The squirrels bumped along off the road, and a road-runner flirted its tail and raced over the edge of the hill and sailed out like a glider.

Jody tried to leap into the middle of his shadow at every step. A stone rolled under his foot and he went down. Around a little bend he raced, and there, a short distance ahead, were his grandfather and the cart. The boy dropped from his unseemly running and approached at a dignified walk.

The horse plodded stumble-footedly up the hill and the old man walked beside it. In the lowering sun their giant shadows flickered darkly behind them. The grandfather was dressed in a black broadcloth suit and he wore kid congress gaiters and a black tie on a short, hard collar. He carried his black slouch hat in his hand. His white beard was cropped close and his white eyebrows overhung his eyes like moustaches. The blue eyes were sternly merry. About the whole face and figure there was a granite dignity, so that every motion seemed an impossible thing. Once at rest, it seemed the old man would be stone, would never move again. His steps were slow and certain. Once made, no step could ever be retraced; once headed in a direction, the path would never bend nor the pace increase nor slow.

When Jody appeared around the bend, Grandfather waved his hat slowly in welcome, and he called, 'Why, Jody! Come down to meet me, have you?'

Jody sidled near and turned and matched his step to the old man's step and stiffened his body and dragged his heels a little. 'Yes, sir,' he said. 'We got your letter only today.'

'Should have been here yesterday,' said Grandfather. 'It certainly should. How are all the folks?'

'They're fine, sir.' He hesitated and then suggested shyly,

'Would you like to come on a mouse hunt tomorrow, sir?'

'Mouse hunt, Jody?' Grandfather chuckled. 'Have the people of this generation come down to hunting mice? They aren't very strong, the new people, but I hardly thought mice would be game for them.'

'No, sir. It's just play. The haystack's gone. I'm going to drive out the mice to the dogs. And you can watch, or even beat the hay a little.'

The stern, merry eyes turned down on him. 'I see. You don't eat them then. You haven't come to that yet.'

Jody explained, 'The dogs eat them, sir. It wouldn't be much like hunting Indians, I guess.'

'No, not much—but then later, when the troops were hunting Indians and shooting children and burning teepees, it wasn't much different from your mouse hunt.'

They topped the rise and started down into the ranch cup, and they lost the sun from their shoulders. 'You've grown,' Grandfather said. 'Nearly an inch, I should say.'

'More,' Jody boasted. 'Where they mark me on the door, I'm up more than an inch since Thanksgiving even.'

Grandfather's rich throaty voice said, 'Maybe you're getting too much water and turning to pith and stalk. Wait until you head out, and then we'll see.'

Jody looked quickly into the old man's face to see whether his feelings should be hurt, but there was no will to injure, no punishing nor putting-in-your-place light in the keen blue eyes. 'We might kill a pig,' Jody suggested.

'Oh, no! I couldn't let you do that. You're just humouring me. It isn't the time and you know it.'

'You know Riley, the big boar, sir?'

'Yes. I remember Riley well.'

'Well, Riley ate a hole into that same haystack, and it fell down on him and smothered him.'

'Pigs do that when they can,' said Grandfather.

'Riley was a nice pig, for a boar, sir. I rode him sometimes, and he didn't mind.'

A door slammed at the house below them, and they saw Jody's mother standing on the porch waving her apron in welcome. And they saw Carl Tiflin walking up from the barn to be at the house for the arrival.

The sun had disappeared from the hills by now. The blue smoke from the house chimney hung in flat layers in the purpling ranch-cup. The puff-ball clouds, dropped by the falling wind, hung listlessly in the sky.

Billy Buck came out of the bunkhouse and flung a wash basin of soapy water on the ground. He had been shaving in mid-week, for Billy held Grandfather in reverence, and Grandfather said that Billy was one of the few men of the new generation who had not gone soft. Although Billy was in middle age, Grandfather considered him a boy. Now Billy was hurrying toward the house too.

When Jody and Grandfather arrived, the three were waiting for them in front of the yard gate.

Carl said, 'Hello, sir. We've been looking for you.'

Mrs. Tiflin kissed Grandfather on the side of his beard, and stood still while his big hand patted her shoulder. Billy shook hands solemnly, grinning under his straw moustache. 'I'll put up your horse,' said Billy, and he led the rig away.

Grandfather watched him go, and then, turning back to the group, he said as he had said a hundred times before, 'There's a good boy. I knew his father, old Mule-tail Buck. I never knew why they called him Mule-tail except he packed mules.'

Mrs. Tiflin turned and led the way into the house. 'How long are you going to stay, Father ? Your letter didn't say.'

'Well, I don't know. I thought I'd stay about two weeks. But I never stay as long as I think I'm going to.'

In a short while they were sitting at the white oilcloth table eating their supper. The lamp with the tin reflector hung over the table. Outside the dining-room windows the big moths battered softly against the glass.

Grandfather cut his steak into tiny pieces and chewed slowly. 'I'm hungry', he said. 'Driving out here got my appetite up. It's like when we were crossing. We all got so hungry every night we could hardly wait to let the meat get done. I could eat about five pounds of buffalo meat every night.'

'It's moving around does it,' said Billy. 'My father was a government packer. I helped him when I was a kid. Just the two of us could about clean up a deer's ham.'

'I knew your father, Billy,' said Grandfather. 'A fine man he was. They called him Mule-tail Buck. I don't know why except he packed mules.'

'That was it,' Billy agreed. 'He packed mules.'

Grandfather put down his knife and fork and looked around the table. 'I remember one time we ran out of meat—' His voice dropped to a curious low sing-song, dropped into a tonal groove the story had worn for itself. 'There was no buffalo, no antelope, not even rabbits. The hunters couldn't even shoot a coyote. That was the time for the leader to be on the watch. I was the leader, and I kept my eyes open. Know why ? Well, just the minute the people began to get hungry they'd start slaughtering the team oxen. Do you believe that ? I've heard of parties that just ate up their draft cattle. Started from the middle and worked towards the ends. Finally they'd eat the lead pair, and then the wheelers. The leader of a party had to keep them from doing that.'

In some manner a big moth got into the room and circled the hanging kerosene lamp. Billy got up and tried to clap it between his hands. Carl struck with a cupped palm and caught the moth and broke it. He walked to the window and dropped it out.

'As I was saying,' Grandfather began again, but Carl interrupted him. 'You'd better eat some more meat. All the rest of us are ready for our pudding.'

Jody saw a flash of anger in his mother's eyes. Grandfather picked up his knife and fork. 'I'm pretty hungry, all right,' he said 'I'll tell you about that later.'

When supper was over, when the family and Billy Buck sat in front of the fireplace in the other room, Jody anxiously watched Grandfather. He saw the signs he knew. The bearded head leaned forward; the eyes lost their sternness and looked wonderingly into the fire; the big lean fingers laced themselves on the black knees. 'I wonder,' he began, 'I just wonder whether I ever told you how those thieving Piutes drove off thirty-five of our horses.'

'I think you did,' Carl interrupted. 'Wasn't it just before you went up into the Tahoe country?'

Grandfather turned quickly towards his son-in-law. 'That's right. I guess I must have told you that story.'

'Lots of times,' Carl said cruelly, and he avoided his wife's eyes. But he felt the angry eyes on him, and he said, ' 'Course I'd like to hear it again.'

Grandfather looked back at the fire. His fingers unlaced and laced again. Jody knew how he felt, how his insides were collapsed and empty. Hadn't Jody been called a Big-Britches that very afternoon? He arose to heroism and opened himself to the term Big-Britches again. 'Tell about Indians,' he said softly.

Grandfather's eyes grew stern again. 'Boys always want to hear about Indians. It was a job for men, but boys want to hear about it. Well, let's see. Did I ever tell you how I wanted each wagon to carry a long iron plate?'

Everyone but Jody remained silent. Jody said, 'No. You didn't.'

'Well, when the Indians attacked, we always put the wagons in a circle and fought from between the wheels. I thought that if every wagon carried a long plate with rifle holes, the men could stand the plates on the outside of the wheels when the wagons

were in the circle and they would be protected. It would save lives and that would make up for the extra weight of the iron. But of course the party wouldn't do it. No party had done it before and they couldn't see why they should go to the expense. They lived to regret it, too.'

Jody looked at his mother, and knew from her expression that she was not listening at all. Carl picked at a callus on his thumb and Billy Buck watched a spider crawling up the wall.

Grandfather's tone dropped into its narrative groove again. Jody knew in advance exactly what words would fall. The story droned on, speeded up for the attack, grew sad over the wounds, struck a dirge at the burials on the great plains. Jody sat quietly watching Grandfather. The stern blue eyes were detached. He looked as though he were not very interested in the story himself.

When it was finished, when the pause had been politely respected as the frontier of the story, Billy Buck stood up and stretched and hitched his trousers. 'I guess I'll turn in,' he said. Then he faced Grandfather. 'I've got an old powder horn and a cap and ball pistol down to the bunkhouse. Did I ever show them to you?'

Grandfather nodded slowly. 'Yes, I think you did, Billy. Reminds me of a pistol I had when I was leading the people across.' Billy stood politely until the little story was done, and then he said, 'Good night,' and went out of the house.

Carl Tiflin tried to turn the conversation then. 'How's the country between here and Monterey? I've heard its pretty dry.'

'It is dry,' said Grandfather. 'There's not a drop of water in the Laguna Seca. But it's a long pull from '87. The whole country was powder then, and in '61 I believe all the coyotes starved to death. We had fifteen inches of rain this year.'

'Yes, but it all came too early. We could do with some now.' Carl's eye fell on Jody. 'Hadn't you better be getting to bed?'

Jody stood up obediently. 'Can I kill the mice in the old haystack, sir?'

'Mice? Oh! Sure, kill them all off. Billy said there isn't any good hay left.'

Jody exchanged a secret and satisfying look with Grandfather. 'I'll kill every one tomorrow,' he promised.

Jody lay in his bed and thought of the impossible world of Indians and buffaloes, a world that had ceased to be forever. He wished he could have been living in the heroic time, but he knew he was not of heroic timber. No one living now, save possibly Billy Buck, was worthy to do the things that had been done. A race of giants had lived then, fearless men, men of a staunchness unknown in this day. Jody thought of the wide plains and of the wagons moving across like centipedes. He thought of Grandfather on a huge white horse, marshalling the people. Across his mind marched the great phantoms, and they marched off the earth and they were gone.

He came back to the ranch for a moment, then. He heard the dull rushing sound that space and silence make. He heard one of the dogs, out in the doghouse, scratching a flea and bumping his elbow against the floor with every stroke. Then the wind rose again and the black cypress groaned and Jody went to sleep.

He was up half an hour before the triangle sounded for breakfast. His mother was rattling the stove to make the flames roar when Jody went through the kitchen. 'You're up early,' she said. 'Where are you going?'

'Out to get a good stick. We're going to kill the mice today.'

'Who is "we"?'

'Why, Grandfather and I.'

'So you've got him in it. You always like to have someone in with you in case there's blame to share.'

'I'll be right back,' said Jody. 'I just want to have a good stick ready for after breakfast.'

He closed the screen door after him and went out into the cool blue morning. The birds were noisy in the dawn and the ranch cats came down from the hill like blunt snakes. They had been hunting gophers in the dark, and although the four cats were full of gopher meat, they sat in a semi-circle at the back door and mewed piteously for milk. Double-tree Mutt and Smasher moved sniffing along the edge of the brush, performing the duty with rigid ceremony, but when Jody whistled, their heads jerked up and their tails waved. They plunged down to him, wriggling their skins and yawning. Jody patted their heads seriously, and moved on to the weathered scrap pile. He selected an old broom handle and a short piece of inch-square scrap wood. From his pocket he took a shoelace and tied the ends of the sticks loosely together to make a flail. He whistled his new weapon through the air and struck the ground experimentally, while the dogs leaped aside and whined with apprehension.

Jody turned and started down past the house towards the old haystack ground to look over the field of slaughter, but Billy Buck sitting patiently on the back steps, called to him, 'You better come back. It's only a couple of minutes till breakfast.'

Jody changed his course and moved toward the house. He leaned his flail against the steps. 'That's to drive the mice out,' he said. 'I'll bet they're fat. I'll bet they don't know what's going to happen to them today.'

'No, nor you either,' Billy remarked philosophically, 'nor me, nor anyone.'

Jody was staggered by this thought. He knew it was true. His imagination twitched away from the mouse hunt. Then his mother came out of the back porch and struck the triangle, and all thoughts fell in a heap.

Grandfather hadn't appeared at the table when they sat down. Billy nodded at his empty chair. 'He's all right? He isn't sick?'

'He takes a long time to dress,' said Mrs. Tiflin. 'He combs his whiskers and rubs up his shoes and brushes his clothes.'

Carl scattered sugar on his mush. 'A man that's led a wagon train across the plains has got to be pretty careful how he dresses.'

Mrs. Tiflin turned on him. 'Don't do that, Carl! Please don't!' There was more of threat than of request in her tone. And the threat irritated Carl.

'Well, how many times do I have to listen to the story of the iron plates, and the thirty-five horses? That time's done. Why can't he forget it, now it's done?' He grew angrier while he talked, and his voice rose. 'Why does he have to tell them over and over? He came across the plains. All right! Now it's finished. Nobody wants to hear about it over and over.'

The door into the kitchen closed softly. The four at the table sat frozen. Carl laid his mush spoon on the table and touched his chin with his fingers.

Then the kitchen door opened and Grandfather walked in. His mouth smiled tightly and his eyes were squinted. 'Good morning,' he said, and he sat down and looked at his mush dish.

Carl could not leave it there. 'Did—did you hear what I said?'

Grandfather jerked a little nod.

'I don't know what got into me, sir. I didn't mean it. I was just being funny.'

Jody glanced in shame at his mother, and he saw that she was looking at Carl, and that she wasn't breathing. It was an awful thing that he was doing. He was tearing himself to pieces to talk like that. It was a terrible thing to him to retract a word, but to retract it in shame was infinitely worse.

Grandfather looked sidewise. 'I'm trying to get right side up,' he said gently. 'I'm not being mad. I don't mind what you said, but it might be true, and I would mind that.'

'It isn't true,' said Carl. 'I'm not feeling well this morning. I'm sorry I said it.'

'Don't be sorry, Carl. An old man doesn't see things sometimes. Maybe you're right. The crossing is finished. Maybe it should be forgotten, now it's done.'

Carl got up from the table. 'I've had enough to eat. I'm going to work. Take your time, Billy!' He walked quickly out of the dining-room. Billy gulped the rest of his food and followed soon after. But Jody could not leave his chair.

'Won't you tell any more stories?' Jody asked.

'Why, sure I'll tell them, but only when—I'm sure people want to hear them.'

'I like to hear them, sir.'

'Oh! Of course you do, but you're a little boy. It was a job for men, but only little boys like to hear about it.'

Jody got up from his place. 'I'll wait outside for you, sir. I've got a good stick for those mice.'

He waited by the gate until the old man came out on the porch. 'Let's go down and kill the mice now,' Jody called.

'I think I'll just sit in the sun, Jody. You go kill the mice.'

'You can use my stick if you like.'

'No, I'll just sit here a while.'